■ ■ ■

BITING SILENCE

BITING SILENCE

Arturo von Vacano

Para Indiana,
con la amistad de
[signature] 03

Ruminator Books
ST. PAUL, MINNESOTA

Published by Ruminator Books
1648 Grand Avenue
St. Paul, Minnesota 55105

www.ruminator.com

10 9 8 7 6 5 4 3 2 1
First Ruminator Books printing 2003

Originally published as *Morder el Silencio* by Ediciones del
Instituto Boliviano de Cultura
First English translation published by Avon Books, 1987
The author has made minor changes to the original translation.

ISBN: 1-886913-58-7
Library of Congress Catalog Number: 87-91163

Cover design by Stewart A. Williams
www.sawdesign.com
Book design by Wendy Holdman
Typesetting by Stanton Publication Services, St. Paul, Minnesota

Printed in the United States of America

■ ■ ■

Para Marcela.
Como siempre.
Como todo.

■ ■ ■

This is fiction.
It has to be fiction:
I am fiction.

■ ■ ■

BITING SILENCE

ZERO

■■■ 1

"What was it like?" asks Julio.

There were two cells, that's all, I thought. And they never hit me, I insisted. There were three children, that's all, I said to myself. And they never stopped loving me, I maintained. There were the dead. There were friends, I remembered. And only one turned out to be a Judas, René, I told myself. There was nothing more. No more was necessary, either.

Every day I went back and forth from the house to the typewriter. Sometimes I stayed out late, drinking. They were born because we wanted them and we loved them dearly. They came out beautiful, intelligent, good. I spent two days in the bigger cell. They never hit me, Julio. I'm telling you.

No one spoke to me nor was I allowed to speak to anyone. Once a guard came into the cell and nearly kicked me, but he realized he was stepping on my head and pulled back his boot and said, "Sorry, *señor*." It's nothing, son, I answered, because in a cell you always sleep with one eye open.

That was all, Julio.

Two cells and three children.

And the siren song.

▪▪▪ 2

I was riding down in the elevator. Flaco said:

"So then, are you still writing?"

No way, I thought. Whatever for?

I said: "Of course. Of course, it's a bad habit. What other meaning would my life have?"

"What are you working on?"

"Anton."

At home I had forty-three chapters tucked away like the flowers widows save after the funeral, the first forty-three chapters. Forty-three. And they never led anywhere. Nor would they ever lead anywhere.

"That's the important thing," mumbled Flaco before he went out into the street.

Yes, I thought. That's the important thing.

Flaco left, walking with his hands in his pockets and looking down at the pavement. I stood there, looking down at the pavement.

Well, I said, sighing, you've got to keep going.

▪▪▪ 3

"It's not worth dirtying your hands for six thousand dollars," I said to René.

"*Coño,*" the mestizo said. "This house isn't going to collapse in two years. I guarantee it."

"But it's poorly built. It will fall in on my children's heads."

The mestizo yawned. Once again we were on the hill, looking at the city in the distance. The huge pit hummed, an upside-down utopia.

"Here it is, see? All the architects who have seen it have said so. You cheated me. It's an entire life, sixty years of work, your life and your work, that you've just buried with those six thousand stolen dollars."

"*Coño,*" the mestizo said. "Have it your way."

"Counselor," I would say later to my lawyer, "there is no way we are ever going to agree."

I was thinking of my children: when would we have a roof over our heads?

"Counselor, I want justice," I would say.

"*Coño,*" René-the-attorney would say. "What a crook!"

And he would dictate a brief.

One cell.

Huge.

And three children.

▪▪▪ 4

The siren song began with Dumas, Remarque, Hemingway, Kipling, Kant, Hesse.

My father's death freed me of his love.

And with seven thousand and fifty-four days charged to my father's account, I took their fictions seriously and left.

The early days of this story have been noted elsewhere. But there were still three thousand, four hundred and fifty-three days to live before going back to my childhood home.

It is such a long time, it is tedious. So sad a story that I was sick with melancholy.

An experience of seven countries, two periods of exile, one year of glory, and thousands of train-plane-bus-foot-hours for nothing.

When I got back, my brother said, "You haven't changed; you're the same jackass you were before. You haven't even changed your accent."

It's true: I still roll my r's as strongly as I ever did, I have the same look in my eye as I took with me, and the song sounds just as sweet now, when I never see the barber because I don't need him anymore.

Maybe the best way would be to call on the postcard trick again.

■ ■ ■ 5

Five hours after my five days in a cell, a young kid who looked poor but not too poor, was educated but not completely yet, with that familiar flashing look in his eye, came up to me and said:

"You should not be grateful to others. It is we who ought to be grateful to you."

In his left hand he held the clipping, rescued from its wastebasket fate, and he held out his slightly trembling right hand, fearful that I might leave it hanging in the air.

I shook his hand and did not understand anything until I understood it and, two-bit sentimentalist that I am, my eyes welled up with tears.

Two words, a smile, and the new member of my Death Row clan, open of heart and hand after reading my little item, left.

You see, when I got out, I wrote a few lines, "Thanks," and it appeared in the newspaper. It was a short note because the power that be had said to me, as he passed a thumb across his throat, "One more word, just one more word out of you . . ."

For a moment, until things got clearer, I thought that all had not been in vain, that the door was still open, a little.

■ ■ ■ 6

Well, hell; on my worktable I have a quotation that says, word for word, "Critics are to literature as eunuchs are to a harem. They know perfectly well what is going on, but they can't get in on it."

And that's how it is, that's all. How am I supposed to pay attention to form now, if soon I will be up to my neck in shit?

But then, why publish what you write for yourself, neither intending to win prizes nor hoping to appear on page 516 of the next *Summary of National Literature*?

And there is also respect for the reader.

The poor thing has to find the leaves, uncover the radish, nibble the little seeds, and even taste the salad.

Forgive me, reader: I have no excuse for stitching and backstitching in this manner except the yearning to discover, damn it all, whether restitching is still possible.

"What other meaning would my life have?" Etc., etc.

In addition, and on the other hand, books of the old school are out of fashion now: nowadays the thing to be is a juggler of words. Or to make movies.

Although, and in the end: forgive me, reader, my friend. My patient, kind, unknown friend:

You are part of it, too.

▪▪▪ 7

"What was it like?" asks Julio.

The thing is, it's painful. This is no way to live. The routine is so routine. The stupidity so stupid. So deadly. Hope so hopeless. Opportunities so lacking.

He says: You're not being coherent. If you hold to your truth, you must speak it, even though speaking it costs you your neck.

I say: But don't you see? It's not my head, it's my little ones' . . .

His verdict: Minutiae, minutiae . . .

I am convulsed as if jolted by an electric shock. If I tell

the truth, it's not my hunger, it's my children's. If I don't speak my truth, I lose the desire to live, life is nothing.

"The meaning my life has . . ."

What's more: these routinarizers are so brutish that after chopping off my head, tchook! They will burn my kind and scatter my ashes in the dust, and then go on being as brutish as ever. That's why you want me to be coherent?

Julio says: Minutiae.

I say: I have an itch but I don't know how to scratch it.

We say: Cheers!

■■■ 8

About Children: We all know, my Fellow Fathers, that children are among the worst investments; just when you need them, they are off in London.

That's fine: some things do not stand to reason; when I was a child, my father tried so hard to make me happy that he literally died from his efforts.

He was honest. And there is nothing more idiotic than a man who is honest and poor.

That is why he died.

But, as Vigil says: "Manhood must be resolved by the child; as an adult, the problem is solved. Right or wrong, it is already solved."

Mimi: "Mommy makes me maple muffins."

We perpetrate pampering on our children until they grow up and perpetrate the same on their own, passing off their pampering as moments of happiness. And the cycle continues.

We, countrymen, are champions when it comes to inflicting happiness on our children. We perform extenuating permutations to make sure that the veil will never, ever be lifted from their eyes and they will never understand the Great Dung Heap they will live in as adults. Or we bury children, our own and others', in the Great Dung Heap, with remarkable indifference.

Then we shout: Long live our homeland, *carajo*!*
And, once a year: Like hell we'll say uncle, *carajo*!
We have plenty of *carajos*. A half plus one.
Oh, yes: Minutiae!

■ ■ ■ 9

Please refer to Appendix A.

I called him Leo because he was too inconsequential to have such a long name. He came into my life between August and January.

He did not keep his word, not even one of the words we tried to use to found a friendship.

Leo the Graduate is another factor to be considered. It is no simple matter to sign a document in triplicate, chatter like a parrot without pausing for air, have one tin ear, and charge people for doing nothing.

It is even less simple to continue doing this for some forty-odd years.

Leo is a bureaucrat.

As such, he drives someone else's car, a car with Official Plates that belongs to his office. He eats breakfast, lunch, and dinner for free, at the office. Even on Sundays.

But he has his own home already; he built a house, nearly destroying a hospital. Someone else's hospital. A state hospital, of course.

Leo is the victim of enormous frustration. He vents it on women. The floor of the official car Leo drives is littered with condoms.

Leo is the work and wisdom of the *Sacrosanta* of April '52.

---

*penis

The Big One. The Real Thing. The Revolution with a capital R.

As he says: My father was a worker and, what's worse, Chilean.

Leo's family has displayed great social mobility.

His father dug ditches. He worked. Leo doesn't now. Leo steals; it's a full-time job.

Ask Gonzalo. And Eliza, who found out about his phony commissions . . . And ask. But enough: that is what the *Sacrosanta* of April '52 has given us.

A world of Leos.

College graduates, lawyers, bureaucrats, bureaucrats, bureaucrats.

Armchair militiamen.

April '52 was supposed to create a New Citizen.

Instead, it gave us an endless supply of perfumed little men who copy Yankee fashions and keep their nails, like ladies' nails, well manicured.

They steal with silk gloves.

Julio says: "Either you speak your truth . . ."

When it came to Leo, no slick lawyers got in our way.

There is nothing more idiotic than . . . Etc., etc.

▪▪▪ 10

"What was it like?" Julio asks again.

That's all it was. That's all. Two cells, three children. René. An attorney named René. The Colonel. Friends. And the dead.

That's all.

"You're not being coherent. That's the trouble."

"But . . . Such savagery . . . One must say . . . Express oneself . . ."

"Minutiae."

"It's my role. It's my duty . . . It's my work . . . I must . . ."

"You should have thought of these things before. Before the kids, I mean."

"But Julio . . . Must it be like this forever? Forever? Forever?"

"That is how the game is played here. With blood, not with ink. And in the end, what for? Nothing is going to change. And least of all on account of what you're doing: it's not serious. No one reads it. And those who read it don't understand it. And those who understand it take it the wrong way."

"No. Someone has to say it. Someone has to stand up to them. And I am read: lots of people read me. It is not all in vain."

"Minutiae."

"But we can hardly breathe anymore . . .

"Walk in the shadows and remember you have children. That's what I say."

"That's why we inherited the country we inherited."

"If you get killed, the country they inherit will be the same, but how are your children going to eat? It's always been this way, and always will be. You know it. I know it. I don't know why you do these things. Come on, you've got to quit this craziness once and for all."

Is he blind or wearing blinders? Better not to say anything now. He loves me. Besides, he's my only friend. Quiet now. It's so late and the world is so empty that we'd best leave it at that.

"Cheers!"

I have to turn up my coat collar to keep out the freezing night air.

"So then, are you still writing?"

Flaco's echo in the elevator.

"Of course, of course. What other meaning would my life have?"

Because, I swore, it must be in some hidden corner.

In the clouds, in the rain, or in the wind, I said to the shadows, it must be there. In some voice, some book. In a guitar, in some stray phrase. Beneath some stone, behind some flower. It must be there; it must be there.

It must be there, because I still hear it.

ONE

I am the tallest, the one in the middle.

"You are the skinny one, right?"

We wore knickers. And drank papaya soda. My mother sits next to me.

"That's my mother."

My father is on the other end, with glasses and a thin moustache and a big forehead. My father . . .

"A typical middle class family, right?"

"I don't know . . . Is there a middle class in Bolivia?"

"If you're going to start that 'I don't know' and 'I don't remember' stuff, I'd better call Atlas. Atlas!"

How's it going, you brute of a guy. Here the dance commences.

"This is Atlas. If you forget, Atlas hits you. If you deny, Atlas hits you. Do you hit hard, Atlas?"

"That's what I get paid for."

"Sir . . . if a denial is needed, Atlas will have to hit. You want the truth, right? To tell the truth is easy. But if you want something more . . . Atlas will have to hit."

"Who is this woman?"

"My grandmother. I hardly knew her."

The woman with catlike eyes and the menacing smile. Sure I knew her. I buried them both, side by side. Twice.

"And this boy?"

"My brother. I don't even know where he lives. Child-hood quarrels, you know . . ."

"No. I don't know. How is that?"

"Well . . . he thinks more or less like you do."

"Oh, the smart one in the family!"

"If you say so . . ."

▪▪▪ 12

The other egg-shaped heads are my brothers, except for one, who has a round head now, and except for another one, who hadn't been born yet. Although he too was born with an egg-shaped head.

"Who is this man?"

"I don't recall. It's so long ago . . ."

The man standing next to my father is a colleague from the office. He's an SOB who stole my father's job. In the oil and mining ministry, where he walked his via dolorosa.

"He still works in the mining ministry. A fine profes-sional. He never gave us any trouble. And the others?"

The others are relatives on my mother's side. Since they are my mother's relatives, I cannot say they are SOBs too. So I won't say it.

"Where was this picture taken?"

"The place is a country house in Obrajes."

In those days we went down to Obrajes to eat our fill and to play *sapo* and to sunbathe. Spicy chicken. *Chairo.* Green grapes, figs. Sun, eucalyptus, prickly pears. And the big tables where everyone sat.

"That thing in your hand . . . is it a weapon? You like those things then, eh? And you were only a child . . ."

"No, sir, it's not a weapon. It's a toy. I liked it because it fired Ping-Pong balls."

My father popped his colleague in the nose with a Ping-Pong ball. Sometimes I think that is why he stole his job at the mining ministry but it can't be.

"What happened to your father?"

My father died a short while later, angina pectoris. My grandmother died another short while later. Broken heart. My mother kept on living. She always had bad luck.

Now, my father is in my desk drawer. My grandmother is in a metal box, tin rings and all. And my mother is in her house, finally with nothing to do after seventy-five years.

"When did he die?"

"When he was forty-three years old."

I have thought of my father every day for the twenty-four thousand, six hundred days of my life. And not a day goes by that I don't think of him.

"He never gave us any trouble. Was he a good man?"

"He didn't believe in those things. He was an honest man. That's common knowledge."

He never learned how to steal, never.

"He doesn't look very young . . . He looks older. Sure that's your father?"

"Yes, sir."

I am one thousand days away from being as old as he was when he died.

"And he died? When?"

"I can't recall exactly."

"That's children for you . . . Did you also forget he was a Mason? What else did you forget?"

"I didn't know he was a Mason. What else should I remember?"

I cannot forget that he died wracked by angina pectoris and because he made me terrifically happy.

"And this one, who's this?"

"That's my father, too."

My father.

Before, he was something like Mandrake disguised as a silly angel.

Now, I don't know who he was.

I lived with him for seventy-three hundred days and never discovered who he was.

Though today too I have thought of my father.

"You're the only one of the bunch who is giving us trouble. We'll find out why. The night is young . . . Do you smoke?"

▪▪▪ 13

I am the tallest, the one with a moustache.

My wife is next to me, with a kerchief on her head and looking at the world as if to ask it: What business is it of yours?

My eldest daughter is near me, my youngest daughter next to her, and my son is near his mother. No one wears knickers now.

"And this one, who's she?"

The Bermuda shorts on the girl near my wife are odd. She herself is odd. One day she came to ask me to hide her Cuban boyfriend because Torres, that infantile Communist, had been overthrown.

"A childhood friend of my wife's."

"A guerrilla fighter. She is a guerrilla fighter. Here she is, see this?"

"I barely know her. I only saw her a couple of times. She came to my house seeking refuge. I said no, that I would never endanger my family."

"She said the same thing. After a good beating, but she said it. You are clever: you don't lie when you don't need to lie. But we will get to the bottom of this little affair. We'll get there, right, Atlas?"

"At your service, Boss."

Now she lives with her husband, a Cuban who I never knew was Cuban, in Paris, France, and I tell my friends in the office when they see this old photograph: I am a bigamist.

"This is your family?"

"Yes. That's my family."

■■■ 14

My daughter came into the world exactly as I wanted her: she is blond as the sun, she is happy, she has her father's wild imagination, and she chattered like a magpie even back in kindergarten.

"Your daughter?"

"The eldest."

She is at the head of her class, so I miss half of her chatter, since it's jabbered in French. She takes ballet lessons to stay trim and she is as nervous as a jumping bean. She is very good natured. She laughs and makes us laugh all day long. My daughter is, possibly, still happy.

"How ashamed she will be, daughter of a radical. And this boy?"

"That's my son."

My son came into the world in three seconds. So fast that I didn't manage to smoke a cigarette. We nicknamed him Puma, although Fox would have been better. His cunning gets him everything he wants, and he does not open his mouth unless it's to utter great truths, truths like my brother utters. He looks after himself as if he were an English dandy. He will probably be a doctor. And he could very well be one: he is also the best in his class.

"I bet you've already filled his head with those red ideas."

"Officer . . ."

"My name is Paez."

"Mr. Paez: I never accepted those ideas; to my mind, Communism is not a valid solution. I do not believe in Communism. And I must say so, even if Atlas works me over."

"It says here that you are a radical."

"What that paper says is not true."

"Even if Atlas works you over?"

"Even so."

"I don't know what to do . . . The President wants you outside, but the Colonel wants you . . . well, the Colonel doesn't like you at all, not one bit. The real truth, I swear on the cross."

"The Colonel?"

"The Boss, then. Or don't you know that, either?"

"I only write stories, Mr. Paez. I know nothing about this. I am a poet, I tell fables. Politics doesn't interest me; I like fiction, I am an existentialist."

"But: what instructions do you receive from abroad? Which do you follow? Who gives you your orders?"

"What do you mean? I don't understand. . ."

"Oh, I think Atlas is going to get to work."

"But it's true: I don't understand you!"

"Well, then, I am going to eat. But I will see you in an hour . . . all right? Atlas: don't break any bones. You know what to do."

■■■ 15

My baby daughter is still very little.

Atlas is smoking, so you relax.

My daughter heard us say she was the little devil of the house and she tries to be one so as not to make liars of us. But you can't see her clearly in this picture. I wonder how much Atlas gets paid. Relax, relax: so far, so good. Look at the picture. How did they get the picture? It was in my desk, at the office. Is this the same one? Yes. I wonder what they did to Lourdes. You: continue.

Remember, savor your days, distract your fear. Note: my daughter has broken fourteen expensive vases, a flower vase that was a hundred years old, a present from my mother, countless cups, jars, pots, and her own head, twice, though it wasn't anything serious. Natalia was calm. But is she free? When my baby daughter went to Cochabamba, she forgot about me, and she called me uncle for a time, until she could place me again. She was two years old here.

If they tortured that girl . . . Hold on, man: steady. Strength. Faith. A little humility . . .

"Mr. Atlas, could I smoke a cigarette?"

"The cigarettes are there. On the table."

"Thank you, Mr. Atlas."

Now we're talking. You relax, relax. Don't even think. Point and indicate: my wife does not walk by my side, but she sometimes keeps in step. She has been with me for forty-four hundred days, minus seven hundred and twenty, the time she needed to visit Cochabamba, her birthplace, and to recharge her batteries. Yes, but if they grab her . . . No, man, no. They won't grab her. Why should they grab her? Any reason will do, you know. Oh, shut up now. Look at the picture and don't think, I'm telling you.

Look, remember, comment: Natalia has done everything humanly possible to make ours a happy home, and she has nearly succeeded. The problem is that we each have a different idea of what a happy home is, Mr. Paez, Mr. Paez, Mr. Paez. Later, if you get out, don't forget Mr. Paez.

But it is the same for us, Mr. Paez, as for many people: bad with you, worse without you. Smoothing over the rough spots, we have built something fairly solid by virtue of vigor. So that sometimes I tell her: you'll be my widow. It sounds prophetic.

"I have thought of my children for thirty-four hundred days."

"Huh?"

"No, nothing, Mr. Atlas."

▪▪▪ 16

I close my eyes and see them at the window when I come home from work, in the afternoon. Three little heads leaning out the window. Six eyes clear as the sky. A cascade of laughter. And their arms around my neck.

Who would they live with if I don't come back? They would go to Cochabamba, with their grandfather, that's for certain. But my daughter, how will they explain to her . . . I am indebted to my children for a second and long-lasting period of happiness. I am so happy with them that sometimes I forget my aspirations, I told Natalia then.

But I remember Flaco, "What other meaning would my life have?," and neither my children nor my placid happiness is enough.

I listen to the song and feel uneasy.

From far away, the humming of the city reaches my ears and I shake my head. The community trembles and I feel like I've left an empty space.

Man was not born to be happy.

"Well, well. Here we are again. Let's see: who is this girl? Don't talk too fast, because I have to write it down. Atlas, go eat now."

▪▪▪ 17

"But . . . why did you become a radical?"

"You mean . . . a reporter? 'The siren song began with Dumas, Remarque, Hemingway, Kipling, Kant, Hesse.'"

"Slow down! Don't you see I have to write it all down? Oh, hell! All foreigners! 'Remark' . . . who else?"

"But no: they are writers. You don't need to note them."

"I have to write it all down. Those are orders. Repeat."

"Hemingway, Kipling . . . Kant . . . Hesse. Yes. That's it, more or less."

"You'll notice that I am polite. I hope you will also be polite."

"You can be certain of that: I will try my best."

"Well: Answer!"

"I never became a radical."

"Oh, but you're forcing me to put Atlas to work."

"Mr. Paez: even if Atlas works me over, I cannot lie. I never was a radical. I am not now nor have I ever been nor will I ever be one. I don't believe in that struggle."

"You swear?"

"I swear."

"Because everything helps you in this country. Your name, your education, your skin. Even your face helps you, and your strange last name. You could have been a diplomat. A minister. And have left it to us, the police, to wage the struggle that is so long, so poorly paid. Why did you do those things, Don Max?"

"But . . . what things? All I have is one novel to my name. Some newspaper articles . . . Nothing, really. No one knows me."

"Hundreds of people are petitioning the President for your release."

"What?"

"That's right. You will get out early in the morning. Didn't you know?"

"No. How was I to know?"

"Don't people talk, in the cells?"

"Yes, but . . ."

"What you have to do is just confess what you have done."

"Then I'll never get out."

"Maybe you will, feet first."

"Are they going to kill me?"

But my children are still very young, very young.

"Atlas: take him out to the yard. Let him breathe a little. He's turning green, this guy. Just three minutes. Then bring him back."

"I'd rather stay here."

If they're going to do what they did to Tatán, from the third floor, I'd rather it be here.

"No. Nothing will happen. Just go, Don Max. Go ahead, I'll wait for you here. Atlas: get me a cup of coffee."

■■■ 18

My father's death freed me of his love.

"But then, why? Where from?"

"From this world. I lived for seven thousand days at my father's expense, then I took those fictions seriously and went out on my own search. I never found them."

"Why do you write those lies? No one believes them. But they bother the Colonel."

"Why . . . is the Colonel bothered?"

"Do you think it's insignificant? I have all your articles . . . Do you want me to read them to you?"

"No, you don't need to, Mr. Paez: those articles are a series of jokes, and bad jokes, besides. They can only bring on an amused smile from any authority, anywhere . . . even you yourself . . ."

"The Colonel was fuming . . . believe me, Don Max."

"They weren't even editorials. They were jokes."

"We know the tricks of the disinformers. I know your work, I read your books."

"My books . . ."

"Your novels."

"Fiction. Just fiction, badly built fiction."

"'The early days of this story have been noted else-where. Weakly.'"

"What do you see, to make you write these things?"

"What did I see, what did I see? A continent in tatters, that's what I saw."

"And your trips . . . Why did you travel? Who paid for your trips? Who do you work for?"

"'There were thirty-four hundred days to live before I stepped into my childhood home.'"

"What did you do?"

"'Seven countries, one year of glory, and . . . for nothing.'"

"That's true: for nothing."

"For nothing: I did not manage to write anything serious, anything worth publishing, worth reading."

"So when did you begin this work?"

"'I made the leap between the high plateau and the sea by plane. But it sounded more romantic if I said I did it on foot. I made the leap across the desert on foot . . .'"

"Slow down, will you? I have to write it all down."

"'. . . foot . . . and I nearly lost life and limb in mid-leap . . . So it sounded rather romantic . . . so . . . I wrote it down . . . as I did.'—"Excuse me, 'sounded' is spelled with 'ou,' not 'ow.'"

"You speak as if you were reciting."

"I am quoting myself. The book everyone refused to publish . . . 'The first one hundred days also sounded romantic so . . . I wrote about them as I lived them.'"

"'Romantic, so'—what?"

"'I wrote about them as I lived them.'—'About' with a 'b' and 'lived' with a 'v'—that's right. Very good."

"It's tiring, to type. I'm going for a walk in the yard. Don't go anywhere, all right?"

"Where could I possibly go, Mr. Paez?"

"It's just an expression, Don Max."

▪▪▪ 19

On public life:

One sunny day of low necklines, a man stops me in the Plaza San Martin and says: "You are the one who writes articles on the commentary page of *Expreso,* aren't you?"

"Yes."

"Congratulations. I always read your articles. Nice job."

"Thanks."

That is how popularity begins.

I am going to bend over backwards to locate Appendix C.

Also on public life:

Ciro Alegria receives me in his house one Saturday afternoon because Manuel Scorza is going to put out another edition of his *Mundo.* I ask my questions and write the article: "From the heights of *El Mundo es Ancho y Ajeno,* Ciro Alegria comes down to . . ." Etc., etc.

I now have a copy of *Mundo Ancho y Ajeno* signed by the author. A lovely dedication.

And more:

Me: "Good afternoon, Don Victor. I'm here for . . ."

Haya de la Torre: "No, please! Don't bother me! You always make me say things I never wanted to say!"

1967:

"Mr. President, about President Kennedy and Vietnam . . ."

Johnson: Next!

Robert Kennedy: I cannot answer that question about President Kennedy and President Johnson . . . You understand why, of course . . .

"Yes, Mr. Kennedy."

1970:

"Senator Mondale, as editor of IBEAS magazine, I would appreciate an article on . . ."

Mondale: I would be glad to write an article for the Bolivians. As to your question about Vietnam . . .

1977:

Me: "Mr. President: The Bolivians are very interested in the priorities of your policy in our country. Would you care to comment?"

Carter: Yes. There are two problems that concern us; human rights must be respected in Bolivia. And two, Americans arrested in Bolivia and charged with drug trafficking must be tried or promptly released.

1977:

"Listen, buddy: I'll sell you an exclusive interview with President Carter for *El Diario:* 'Half an Hour with Carter,' how's that?"

Buddy: "Be glad we'll publish it for you . . . And you want money, too?"

"Thanks, buddy. Ciao."

1973:

"The real cause of this crisis is corruption at the highest levels of government."

The Colonel: Shoot him!

The Law: Lock him up!

1978:

Flaco: "So then, are you still working?"

Me: "Of course; it's a bad habit. What other meaning would my life have?"

The young, intelligent television reporter: "Why aren't you publishing your new work? You haven't published anything in three years, Don Max. Are you afraid of the critics?"

"No, I am afraid of the Beast."

"What did you say? I don't understand."

"Lucky for you."

■■■ 20

On private life:

1960:

Me: If my father had seen what I did it would have killed him . . .

Greta: You're the only man I've ever met who starts crying at a time like this . . . Come on, get down from there!

1961:

Me: My goodness, now I have a steady job and everything. And if you'd like to go out with me tomorrow . . .

Juana del Callao: But, my dear, I'm old enough to be your grandmother . . .

Me: With a grandmother like you, who needs grandchildren?

1963:

Me: That's enough, enough, enough!

Juana: Man, you're mean.

1964:

Sylvia: If you're going to waste my time, I'd rather . . .

Me: But Sylvia, I love you!

1965:

Me: I do, Father.

Natalia: I do, Father.

1966:

Harry: You won it! Congratulations: you'll come to the United States.

Me: Thank you, Harry.

1968:

Me: Hi, Mom.
    Mom: My son!

1969:

Me: This country isn't worth shit.
    Natalia: But it's our country.

1970:

Natalia: We'll name her Eliana . . .
    Me: My God!

1971:

Natalia: We'll name him Alejandro . . .
    Me: Good God!

1973:

Natalia: We'll name her Natalia . . .
    Me: Oh, God!

1974:

Me: I'd like to get back to writing . . .
    Natalia: My God!
    The song.

TWO

■■■ 21

They kept me locked up all day in a big cell with army cots and a partially sunken wooden floor, and it was raining outside. It's for fraud, they had told Natalia at six in the morning when they made me get dressed and follow them. There were eight of them, all armed. Who did they think I was, Che?, my wife said later.

I smoked and smoked, in a navy blue suit, with a coat that was nearly brand new, a suitcase purchased in Panama, a sky blue tie. In my briefcase I had a revolver I'd brought home years before, with the idea that in Bolivia one must have a gun to protect one's home from thieves.

When I remembered the revolver, I broke out in a cold sweat. It was in my briefcase for months because I didn't want the children to find it, play with it, have an accident.

To stall for time, I locked the briefcase and threw the keys down a hole in the floorboard.

My belt, tie, shoelaces, personal papers were confiscated, everything but a handkerchief and money, sunglasses and a comb. I never saw the briefcase again.

"Sometimes they commit suicide," said the guy who made a list of my things. Huanca. He had learned it from television.

Fraud, Huanca said. Swindlers don't ever commit suicide. That was how I found out.

Crime: "The real cause of this crisis is corruption at the highest levels of government."

Place: evening edition, *Ultima Hora*.

Date: two days before.

Corpus delicti: column on commentary page.

Office of National Security: Guilty!

I thought: Oh, poor little scribbler. Here it comes. Now they're going to kick journalism into you. Oh, crabby loudmouth. Start dancing. Now they're going to tell you what you can and can't write. Now it's come to this.

But, it was still the first day.

So I feigned ignorance: "You there: when can I talk to your boss?"

I am still a gentleman, I consoled myself.

They looked at me mutely from across the yard and through the rain.

All day long.

Then I relived the forty-seven hundred and fifty days at the typewriter that had led me to this freezing cell.

I slept in a corner, curled in a ball, shivering at times. I heard nothing but the midnight taxis cruising down the street.

An occasional drunk.

And there was no song.

▪▪▪ 22

How simple and straightforward it all seems when the man on the other side of the bars, the one who is happily playing with a six-shooter, can make a mistake and erase all at once thirty years of books, trips, pleasures, griefs, excesses, and typewriters. And a thousand decades of hope.

You learn easily and quickly how defenseless you are

when you look through a crack in the wooden door and you study (because, really, it was the first time I had him within eye's reach) the man playing with a six-shooter on the other side of the bars.

And what fear, what quivering fright you learn to feel when you finally discover, because you have a wealth of time, that that man is master of your house, your children, your life, your past, your posterity . . .

Him.

How idiotic the bad habit of writing seems then. A yearning, turned foolhardy, to search for solutions. A desire, turned childish, to find the Promised Dawn. A necessary illusion to believe in.

And how clearly old suspicions change into unbearable certainties.

He, who is playing with the six-shooter and whom you, man of letters, have never seen before, is Master of the World.

He is the supreme immortal. Invulnerable, like God. He, who wields his authority without counterfeit cries; silent and confident, indestructible, he is the truth you have been seeking. He was born before the country was born and will die the last day of Eternity.

And you, crippled by an education you believed you had mastered—Columbus discovered America on October 12, the atomic weight of astatine is 210—you are unnecessary. Less than that: you are a stupid annoyance. And worse yet: you will never know how to beat the one who is playing with his six-shooter.

But how, but then, but, but, but.

The hand that plays with typewriters does not easily make a fist.

Ten thousand days earlier, the mind that absorbs pages upon pages had already rejected the idea of the Beast.

For the fortunate child rocked to sleep with Aesop's fables, Snow White, El Cid, things by Verlaine, chapters by Hemingway and the worlds of Ray Bradbury, the Beast had become extinct on the last day of the glyptodon's existence.

But now, through the crack of an old wooden door, you glimpse the glyptodon here, the Beast.

He is master of the world, because everything has been made for him. Immortal, because he has learned to come alive after his own death. Invulnerable because, having no duty other than to himself, who can harm him?

A roof over his head and clothes on his back, the man with the six-shooter plays and looks at the world with the tamed patience of a wild bull in his den.

I smoked like a chimney, trying to let my lesson sink in; for it to sink in would be to deny my very right to live. To accept that the Beast would never, ever go away.

▪▪▪ 23

The Beast did not exist in the little house where seven years of tolerable poverty were blended with small pleasures and childhood joys. The Beast was impossible when books and music and baby feet had come at the same time. The Beast was too disgusting and unbelievable to be conceived by children's eyes.

Until now.

Because now the Beast had wormed its way in before dawn, in between the little footsteps. And the children could not believe their eyes. The guns were not toys and the woman who was crying, collapsed in the corner, was crying as never before, helpless in her anguish.

When the Beast left, taking Daddy away, the children's eyes changed forever. And when Daddy did not come back by sundown, the children's minds recalled the faces of the Beast.

When Mommy began to cry because there was practically nothing else she could do, the children's hearts began to know fear.

Later they began to piece together the new truth, that one must fear the police more than thieves. But then, on television . . .

Months later, a little voice would say in the middle of the night: "When they took you away, Mommy cried . . . and I, I sat in a corner, and cried."

Later my wife would tell me: "He didn't eat. He couldn't sleep. He just lay there. He didn't cry."

When the Beast went to that little house, he showed once again that he draws his breath from fear.

In time he would teach that he feeds on forgetting.

And that he also needs indifference, hypocrisy, and above all, stupidity.

As the days passed, the little feet took firmer steps and reached a time when the Beast was not even an unpleasant memory.

Except in Daddy's guts.

"It's the meaning of my life." Etc., etc.

But, as much of an accomplice as Mommy, Grandma, Grandpa, Aunts and Uncles, Daddy also wanted to erase the Beast, almost entirely, from the children's memories.

And it seemed then that the Beast did not exist.

Only Daddy, who kept saying: it's the song.

■■■ 24

But the Beast exists.

The lesson got learned.

This order of things, then, is possible.

Speeches are also possible.

Absurdity is possible.

The hunger of many is possible, and the satiety of the few.

And the eternal, boring, deadly, monstrous dance recommences.

"Father, into thy hands I commend my spirit."

At least he did not die in such loneliness.

▪▪▪ 25

When I finished traveling around the United States for fourteen months, living like a king, I went to see Harry and asked him for money for another scholarship; behold, the golden dream that would never come true.

"I want to go to school in New York City. A course in creative writing."

Harry gave me another thousand dollars.

At the time we were floating on the Mississippi, so I got off at the next port and took a Greyhound to New York City.

When I arrived at New York University, I discovered that the first thing you have to do is take a proficiency examination.

It was a classroom as big as a stadium, filled with a hundred truckloads of Latin Americans. They all looked like wedding guests. They were out of place: it was not a matter of godparents and betrothals, but of regular and irregular verbs and their differences; no connections or bribes allowed.

To begin with, they hated my red beard, my acrid truck driver stench, without deigning to look at me from the heights of their capillary monuments, their sartorial extravagances, their high-heeled shoes, his and hers. Only the occasional, timid blink of an eye betrayed their fear of yet another failure in that awkward language, so hard and unrefined, that would one day replace the lineage of Cervantian loquacity, the diverse but similar singsong accents that had traveled on their tongues from the Caribbean. Shoulder to shoulder and back to back, they elbowed one another left and right with gusto.

I looked, and was, extremely dirty. These new Americans were no concern of mine. Until then, I had never seen one up close. I had traveled halfway across the country on four Greyhounds, had slept on Greyhounds and eaten french fries and popcorn for five days, buying nougat out the Greyhound bus window. Orangeade. I was scraggly, shaggy, foul-smelling, exhausted.

But I was there. On time.

They put us in rabbit cages with earphones, and riddled us with questions in a printed book.

"When you are ready, press this button."

I sat down, took out my pencil, and began.

"This is the English-language proficiency examination," a Puerto Rican moon-and-palm-tree voice said into the earphone. "Get comfortable. Relax. Begin the test now."

"Open your notebook. Do you see the first question? Write your answer."

Ding.

"Very good. You have three minutes to answer the following questions."

"When you hear the signal, stop work on Part One and go on to Part Two."

Ding.

"This is Part Two. You have three minutes to answer the following questions. Answer as many as you can. If you hear the signal before you have answered them all, go on to Part Three."

Ding.

Now, my nerves surging to the surface, I was perspiring. And I felt an urgent need for a shower.

"Please answer the following questions."

Ding.

"Listen: what is the correct English word for *absolver*? Silence. "Write your answer now."

"Read Part Ten." Silence. "Good. Now, start to translate into English. Stop when you hear the signal."

"Translate now."

Ding.

Ding.

Ding.

We waited afterward shoulder to shoulder, for an hour or so. They were grading the efforts of the crowd that was dressed for a wedding reception. Their scorn was still stinging me, in stray sidelong glances, and I smoked, looking down at the floor.

Finally a voice came over the loudspeaker.

I was first. The first one out of several truckloads of perfumed, bejeweled, freshly showered Latinos. Ninety-nine out of a hundred.

Silently I walked through the crowd, staring at the door to my dreams and disdaining those who were watching me, and I came across a typical career schoolteacher: skinny, short, a goatee, infinitely sad eyes, a cheap raincoat over his arm and a thick book in his hand. *Teacher.* I told him my desire. It was a one-year course and I needed close to two thousand dollars.

"I only have a thousand," I said, and I laid it on the table. The look in his eyes was so sad, I felt sorry for him. I, who had fought and scraped and suffered for six years to get to this moment. Two thousand dollars for the class alone. For a room, for books, for board . . .

"It's not possible, then," I said fatalistically.

"Maybe we can do something for you," he said half hopefully.

But they couldn't. The thousand was there, but there was no "I'll bring the rest tomorrow" or anything of the sort.

I went out, carefully closing the much sought-after door, and found myself in the street. I crossed two avenues, checked into a little hotel, bathed, went to sleep, and ran through the thousand dollars in a week. Drinking.

Later, I worked at dodging Immigration. For a month. Without papers, it was only question of time. But I never tried to be a wetback. False pride.

They had let me sniff the Big Pie but they would never give me a piece of it.

▪▪▪ 26

In the beginning:

It was Peru under Prado, so even the whores were duchesses.

No one could get a decent job unless he was Prado's brother-in-law's cousin's cousin's cousin.

Later, Belaunde came out onto the palace balcony to welcome Velasco's tanks, but I was no longer in Peru then, so I bit my nails, in pure rage, in a little hotel in Philadelphia.

I was not at the Fall of Talara, either, and I bit my knuckles in Albuquerque.

And I missed the earthquake too, so I was very glad to have been spared the sight of Velasco's tanks in Lima or Talara.

But I did live in Peru under Prado—the Old Fag's Viceroyalty, so to speak. Gringo, Zambo, Nano, Germán, Rulito Pinasco, today a famous, congenial, and popular television personality, and Sombra—all lived in Peru under Prado.

We were all good boys and we all, except for Germán,

Nano, and Zambo, went hungry because we were ambitious youths.

The song was in hi-fi and stereo then.

Then came the Queen of England's coronation. José Claudio assigned me to the telex and they couldn't find me under that mountain of paper. José Claudio fired me on the spot, for incompetence. But shortly afterward he rehired me and treated me to a beer in the newspaper lunchroom.

When they discovered I could write a little better than my colleagues, they gave me a desk and a typewriter. I would write at night and sleep during the day. Then I would write at night, drink and talk until dawn, sleep during the day.

Or during the morning, because in the afternoon I would trot around alone like a dog, and without a penny in my pocket.

My first assignment was to spy on the *aprista* students at San Marcos when they were conspiring against Pedro Beltrán, a geezer who thought he was presidential material. I said I was a Bolivian college student passing through Lima and I blithely stepped into that can of worms. I liked the *apristas*. They were like the *movimientistas* only more moderate. They hadn't killed anyone, almost. Apart from the Trujillo affair thirty years before.

I came back with my story to write it up for José Claudio. I wrote it up and immediately discovered the first unwritten law of journalism: Freedom of the press ends on the editor's desk.

But the song was so hi-fi and so stereo that I continued writing about films and about books and about people for Pedro Beltrán until a popular outcry closed down his quite partial newspaper, *El Imparcial*. Politicking rag that it was, having declared bankruptcy before Beltrán—Beltrán was Minister of Finance—Beltrán the publisher would not have to give his reporters severance pay if he fired them.

And he fired us and didn't pay us anything, and I was out on the street again.

That was Peru under Prado.

I saw a jealous Chinese who hung himself from a door jamb and his soft leather shoes hit me in the stomach, I saw a crazy and beautiful woman who composed the sweetest poetry in the world, I saw the faces and knives of anonymous cage-dwellers in dirty police stations. I drank with a German man whose magic fingers broke into the best jazz in the world just for me on a grand piano and, on a deserted beach, I jumped with the brave girls in uniform bellowing their battle cry: *Viva el Peru,* God damn it!

Such was my baptism.

It made the song sound louder.

▪▪▪ 27

I left my tonsils in Peru. Hospital Obrero. Two days. "Say 'ah' for thirty seconds," the doctor said. It felt like he was extracting wisdom teeth from my intestines.

"'Ow di' i' go," I asked afterward.

But, the next day, they said:

"We need the bed."

And that afternoon I dressed, packed my few little things, and went walking to my job.

I had been fired. A matter of gossip and office politics.

I went to my apartment.

It was empty as usual. There was no light.

"Wha' shi'," I said.

▪▪▪ 28

René Ortiz, the mestizo.

Barrel-chested. Olive-skinned. Dirty, cloudy, crafty eyes. Big brown hands. A bullfighter, this man. *"Coño,"* he used to say—and he had friends who were dandies when there still were dandies—because his cape passed close to the bull's neck.

René Ortiz, my friend.

At the age of six he won my trust. Your father was my friend, he said. And my brother, the other one, said: Yes, of course, that's René. And René: When your father was dying, I bought his car. The '36 Buick. Yes, of course: that's René.

René Ortiz, the thief.

"René, you know this is the most important thing in my life. This is the only time I am going to have the money to build a little house. I have three children, you bastard! Don't swindle me . . .

"*Coño.* Have it your way."

René, Counselor, you are our friend. You are famous, invincible, fair, wise, brave, good, honest. Counselor: I want justice. I am poor but I will pay you. Little by little, yes, but I will pay you. Defend the roof over our heads, Counselor.

"Good Lord, man," said René-the-lawyer, "that's an easy one."

Three years and two cells later, I thought: Why didn't he simply refuse? Why didn't he say: "Good Lord, man, I don't have time for petty thievery . . . I make millions fighting million-dollar cases between millionaires . . . Good grief, man: why don't you and your little house go fly a kite?"

I know why. My father was honest. My mother is a lady. And, no matter what I do, I cannot forget my father or my mother: I am naked.

René and René. The thief and the law.

I think: There is nothing more idiotic, more superfluous, more absurd than a man who is honest and poor. Nothing.

Perhaps there is: a man who is honest and poor who cannot learn to be a thief.

Later I walked down the rocky path to the city. It was drizzling.

I mumbled: *Viva la Patria,* God damn it!

▪▪▪ 29

I was looking at the Mountain. The three peaks like white jewels against an indigo, nearly black sky. I was enjoying the warm sun in el Prado. Stationed on trucks, dark figures in red berets and uniforms glared down at their enemies. And those enemies looked down at the pavement, walking on to earn a living.

"Good afternoon, Don Max."

"Good afternoon, Saturnino."

The students. White smocks and red notebooks, just like the ones at the Ministry of the Interior, where I had to sign in every Saturday. The long, green bench.

The old watchman Saturnino's shy smile. His civil service uniform once navy blue, now mended and remended at the elbows and knees.

How does a person get from here, I looked at the students and turned my head, to there, looking at the green and black uniforms, to feeling real hate, primed to kill any passerby, your own father, your own mother . . . How does it happen?

"Saturnino . . . How does a person get to be where they are?"

"I don't know, Don Max. They're always there, patrolling up and down."

"'Children are among the worst investments; just when you need them, they are off in London.'"

"My children went to Santa Cruz, Don Max, not to London."

"'My father made me happy until he died to make me happy.'"

"I just did the best I could; we miners are very poor, Don Max. That's why they left."

"'He was honest, and there is nothing more idiotic than a man who is honest and poor.'"

"God bless your father. He was a fine gentleman."

"That's why he died."

"And your mother was a saint!"

"It is hard to be a saint."

"Don't we know it."

"'An adult man is a problem that has already been solved, for better or worse,' Saturnino. Do you understand me?"

"That's how it is, I guess, Don Max."

"'And the cycle continues.' Do you understand?"

"Yes, it does continue."

"We, dear Saturnino . . . 'are champions at committing solutions against our children: our affection blinds our children; our indifference condemns them, with amazing naturalness, to the Pile of Shit.' Do you understand?"

"Our children forget about us, Don Max. There is no more respect, no . . ."

"Then, we shout: *Viva la Patria,* carajo!"

"That's easy."

"And once a year: Like hell we'll say uncle, carajo!"

"The hero of Topater: brave words, Don Max."

"There are lots of carajos among us."

"You can say that again, Don Max."

Minutiae.

"But someone ought to tell your story of the mine, Saturnino."

"Some day when you're not drinking, Don."

Without the sun, I left el Prado.

Echo: your mother was a saint!

▪▪▪ 30

If "to novelize" is "to make novels," "to nivolize" is "to make nivolas" . . . therefore:

Unamuno: "No novelas: nivolas."

OK, let's *nivolize*:

The afternoon of January 23, eons ago, she arrived at four o'clock, walked in the door of the apartment where I was rotting away in my tee shirt and beard, sprawled out on an old armchair, and she said:

"Hello."

She had come overland, just as she promised, and she found a walking, yellow corpse, a sick and neurotic man who hated the world so much he feared it and resolved to let himself die because suicide hurts.

It was what they call love.

She arrived at a critical moment, to say the least.

After ten thousand and eight hundred hours, the first sentence nearly completed, before returning to the newspaper office, waiting to gather the requisite strength to fight the senseless battles of daily life that keep the gears of the system turning, the man lounging about and spending his days watching an ancient television set and smoking cheap cigarettes did not really seem worthy of being loved.

His nervous system, never terribly resistant, had survived two years of continual insomnia, four hundred and sixty-three days of blacklist and unemployment, eleven thousand, one hundred, and twelve hours of wandering, solitude, and desperation.

And what's more: he hated Lima.

He hated it so much that he could not go down the seven flights of stairs to the street without falling prey to raging vertigo, seasickness, nausea, and thoughts as black as the night.

He was, it must be said, a defeated man.

And he felt a volcano in his stomach when she appeared in the doorway with a suitcase that was not very big and a fresh and sweet smile and she said:

"Hello."

She was, by all accounts, everything the man had lost. Not only that; she was also everything he had left behind the day he had fled his father's house to seek his fortune. Not only that, she was the person who best symbolized the country he had left behind, with the intention of never returning. She was, and it was terrifying, a human being who had not known evil or the system's perversion or cruelty: fresh out of school, she had traveled a bit and what she really was doing was throwing herself into a bottomless sea, not knowing what to expect.

She did not waste time. In three months, she accomplished what six of those specialists that gringos call "shrinks" could not accomplish in two years. She never faltered: she picked up the pieces of the man, cured his dizzy spells, his nausea and black thoughts, took him by the neck, bathed him, worked on his ego, and the day of the miracle arrived: I managed to return to the newspaper office, unswerving of step. To see me from afar, you would not know that anything had gone wrong.

It was what they call love.

Two months later, we got married. At first, it was going to be just her, the priest, and I. Later the entire Bolivian colony appeared. And on the big day I dressed up like an ambassador and said: I do. Three months later, Harry showed up, took me out to eat chicken and drink beer for fourteen hours, and he told me:

"You have won it!"

That day at dawn, back in the thimble we called our apartment, she wept when I told her what I had won.

One month later, at midnight, she flew back home and, crying like a baby, I said good-bye.

Eight hours later, I flew to New York.

It took me six years. I worked for six years to get to New York, and I couldn't do it.

José Claudio needed twelve hours. Harry, fifteen minutes, and she waited for fourteen months.

Then we got back together.

I listened to her song.

But it is no one's fault: it had been written.

What a way to *nivolize*.

THREE

■■■ 31

Dear Daddy,

How are you? We are fine but we miss you a lot and we'll miss you even more at Christmas.

How are you going to spend Christmas there?

We are fine but worried. Grandma is sad and Mommy and Auntie are worried and they cry.

What are you doing there?

We go to the movies and other places with our uncles. Eliana, Natalia, Majanda and me played jungle.

I miss you a lot but I know we will be together soon, but sometimes when I read your letters I get a little sad when I remember that we used to play soccer in the garden. You know, we don't know if the curfew will be lifted for Christmas. And last of all: Merry Christmas!

I send you 100,000,000 kisses.

Your loving son

I can see his face in the dark corner at dawn when I returned home, five days later. I can see his troubled green eyes, and I constantly see the hurt I can never heal.

I see his little knees in the dawning light. I see his little hands trying to protect himself, as he knows already he is defenseless.

I can hear his mother's voice telling me:

"He didn't eat. He couldn't sleep. He just lay there. He didn't cry."

And I always dream about him.

I dream about my child and sometimes wake up shouting.

■■■ 32

Two months after I got my working papers in Peru, I was working as assistant to the editor in chief of *Expreso*. I was also in the press section at the British Embassy. Since I had some money, I invited Mom and little Egghead— the one who hadn't been born yet when the picture was taken—to Huampani for the summer. I wanted to end five years of living in exile by announcing my next ten years of wandering.

Four days before their arrival, *Expreso* had me translate a saucy story about Belaunde and his secretary, a piece that had appeared in the German magazine *Stern*. I did it quickly, laughing as I worked, because the *Stern* comment concerned Belaunde's affair with his secretary, a well-known secret about the President.

The editor in chief okayed it and did not change even one comma—by then, even I had forgotten I was not Peruvian—and sent it off to the printer.

The Sunday the German translation was due to come out, government troops invaded the shop, destroyed the plates halfway through the printing, and ordered that the space reserved for Belaunde's gonads be filled instead with a picture of Sophia Loren.

The day that Mom and Egghead arrived in Lima, I

went to the *Expreso* office at noon and found my dismissal notice. At three o'clock I went to the British Embassy and found my British dismissal notice.

I used my public relations smile number two that night to welcome Mom and Egghead.

That was another unwritten rule of journalism: Freedom of the press dies on the editor's desk, but the errors are the fault of the copywriter.

In other words, the chief is wrong, but he is right.

For fourteen months, no one would give me a job.

Belaunde's affair with his secretary made a "Communist" out of me.

Later, Belaunde married his secretary. What *Stern* had commented on was common knowledge all over Peru.

But I had translated the story. The editor in chief was Panza Reyes, who had been born in Peru, not Bolivia.

Ergo: good-bye.

I was so young then that the song sounded like Maria Callas singing.

▪▪▪ 33

If you think my opinion of Peru has changed on account of that experience, you are wrong.

Years later, when I gave an open class in journalism, a chubby, mischievous boy with a clean, sincere look came up to me after class one day and said:

"I found out that Che Guevara's entire Bolivian campaign was waged with maps that the officers of the chief of staff in Miraflores gave him when he infiltrated their headquarters in disguise.

I wrote up the story and gave it to my editor and it appeared in *El Diario* the following day.

Then the Office of National Security locked me up for a month.

The siren.

That is why I never wanted to be editor in chief.

But when the authorities denied me my papers in Peru and no one wanted to lend me a hand, Washington Chirinos, an editor from *La Prensa,* helped me until my papers came through.

After that, the Conquest of Lima was no sweat.

When I wrote: "The real cause of this crisis is corruption at the highest levels of government," the editor of my paper was the one who got me out of jail.

My wife and him.

Other people I knew helped, but it was mostly his and my wife's efforts that got me out of the cells.

In spite of a liar who had stirred up bad blood between us so we could never be the friends we had been before.

I always missed him a little.

That's how it goes.

Because of this kind of people, I always wanted to be a journalist.

Always, although it is impossible.

I mean, to be the kind of journalist I wanted to be.

▪▪▪ 34

Let's *nivolize*:

I flew in from O'Hare. I had breakfast at Kennedy. I shaved in a public bathroom where you have to pay twenty-five cents to relieve yourself, and I saw a constant stream of old geezers who spied on everyone else's pecker. I paid a dollar to leave my suitcase in a relatively safe place. I went out for some fresh air and the cold hurt my chest.

I returned to the huge room. I had an ice cream. I ate a hamburger; "Mommy says everything there tastes like plastic." I remembered Ana Anita Ana. A Coca-Cola. A pack of Lucky Strikes. I thought of calling Harry. Then

I thought better of it. People only receive you if they are ready to see you . . . otherwise, they don't. Always remember: you are sophisticated now. Harry won't be home and I knew that would make me sadder.

I remembered a nice lady from Peru. No, she wouldn't even remember my name, I thought. I searched my memory for a friend in New York. I tried to picture the face of that other guy, the huge Japanese guy, kind as a saint, sentimental as an old lady, whom I will never forget because once, when he was drunk, he tried to kill me with a karate chop to the neck. In a bar. Karate. Karate in Kentucky. Good title for something. A blow that downed a rather solid mediator. Great blow, Ko, my friend . . . His name was Ko, I realized. He said he was sorry afterward, but he could have killed me. But he didn't kill you. But . . . Oh, fine, finish it. I didn't know where to call him. Nor would I know what to say to him. In the heart of the biggest city in the world, I had no one to talk to.

"It's cold here."

The old lady spoke almost reproachfully, not looking at me. One of those little old ladies who abound on the corners, in the bus stops, in the downtown areas and malls of America.

"Sorry," I said, feeling foolish.

"My rheumatism didn't cut up last year, but that was because Nick was home . . . Then he left. He got married, and now I never see him. Personally, I never liked the girl. She isn't bad but I didn't like her. I told Mike: 'It's better not to get married.' But Nick got married, he went away, and now I never see him."

"Who is Mike?"

"Nick's brother."

"Who is Nick, your son?"

"No, my children live in California. Nick is the doorman. He was the doorman at the house."

"Oh, the doorman."

"He's black of course . . . But sometimes I need someone to talk to. And Nick was always well mannered. He never smelled bad."

"That's good."

"Of course that's good. Mike stinks."

"I thought that was just a prejudice people have."

"No, it's true, they smell bad. All of them. All except Nick."

"Maybe that's why he got married."

"No. She knew that Nick had a thousand dollars in the bank."

"I don't believe you."

"Oh, yes. When he brought her to the house, I told her so myself. I studied her reaction. Nick is hard working, I told her, and he's responsible: he doesn't drink or run around chasing black girls. Nick is a good guy. You can bet on Nick."

"Well. A black guy has to chase black girls, doesn't he? It's only natural."

"Not nowadays."

"Not nowadays?"

"That's right. Things have changed a lot. This country has gone to the dogs. No one remembers Saint Thomas Moriarty anymore. No one says novenas anymore. We are morally dead. And these things are so harmful."

"What, black guys chasing black girls?"

"No."

She looked at me and blinked like a cat. She hunted for a cigarette in a gigantic, ugly plastic bag, carefully placed it in a white holder, and eventually lit it with a lighter, which she took pains to search for inside that immensity. She opened her mouth to say something and then clamped it shut, turned herself off, her eyes clouding over like the burnt-out bulbs of a transistor radio.

She turned herself off, she looked quietly at the hospital-green walls and smoked, and I wanted to go snap! with my fingers, to get her going again, for this tiny, wrinkled old lady was better than being there alone, thinking of going back home, but she had decided that I had never existed, was not even there. I looked around and saw many more like her, old orphans of the night who take refuge in the shifting mists of bad memories. They are called little old ladies. Little old ladies with gigantic plastic and paper bags. Leftover pieces of . . .

"I'm dead, too."

"Excuse me!"

She looked at me from under her wide-brimmed straw hat, got up, and walked away, her arm at an aggressive angle, her cigarette menacing the passersby. I scratched the tip of my nose, crossed my legs, started playing with a loose thread of my sock.

"He's a son of a bitch. A bastard. But he's great in bed."

"You don't love him. Why don't you leave him?"

"I don't know. Where would I go? I don't know what to do."

"You don't love him, do you?"

"I don't know. He's great in bed, but how are you supposed to know it if you love a guy?"

"I don't believe you."

"Yeah. I'll go back out to the coast now, I'll see him, we'll get it on and I'll be satisfied, but I won't be happy."

"No one is happy."

I got up and started to stroll. America is a huge, empty shell. Americans have transistorized eyes, automatic stomachs; their hearts work on batteries. They eat plastic, disguised as fried eggs, and they are empty inside, like chocolate dolls. That time we were with Luigi in Georgia, everyone looked pale, mumbled in monosyllables and eyed us as if they were about to attack. Plain broth and dry bread, two dollars. If they ate *aji* they would be friend-lier. But they are not unfriendly, either. It's that they do not develop some areas of their daily lives. They are empty shells. So, who cares?

Remember 42nd Street . . . Seven weeks on 42nd Street, from one to six in the morning because you couldn't sleep. The crazies every six minutes, day and night. There is this guy with the imaginary yo-yo, darting like a bullfighter at high speed in between the cars, agile and elegant and dashing, sporty hat and moustache, a suave, sweet-looker, if a bit sly, and his fantasy yo-yo flying half a mile up each time he tosses it. He sees it, feels it, smells it, talks to it, takes care of it, and it doesn't exist. Like the old lady back there. Or like me, now. And the other one who also walked with the greatest speed, so gentlemanly and courteous, beauti-ful Irish beard, red and copious, flowing onto his floral print multi-colored shirt, under the coquettish school-teacher hat of fish and flowers, and the enormous pin. Every man and his yo-yo. What a pain in the . . . I don't have a yo-yo. I never had a yo-yo. Unless you count Ravic. Ravic, Robert Jordan, and the leopard.

The sun, made of neon today, disappears at three in the afternoon. It has begun to snow and the little win-dowpanes look sad and pale, like prison oxeyes. These windows are meant to hide, they are not made to look into a broad alien world. This all looks bad, it's as if everybody were going to die soon. Night falls all of a sudden, faster than an amen. Amen: priests, in the shadows of sin, a light that saves us, a feeble light . . . That priest was gay, he was. What must never be lost are the shadows. Shadows have always reigned among us. Down here, when man looks within or looks about; beyond, up there, when he goes into outer space. An immense and silent sea of shad-ows. Inner world, outer world, black worlds. The light of hope, my son . . . Like rag dolls we hang on to rituals.

The light recedes, we are getting accustomed to living without it, we are learning to live without it in our mechanical puppet show.

"A cup of coffee, please."

Cold, liquid plastic.

The machine orders with a loud voice: gate number four. The puppets stand up and move forward, half-blindly, trusting to fate, which will line them up. They get in line, the plane swallows them up, they fly away and line up to get off and go outside to take taxis that are waiting in line and . . .

The thing about sex is that there aren't many possible variations.

I still have four more hours.

We can wait in the lounge. Lounge, lounge. Taste the word. Exotic.

Ravic.

Me.

Oh, for a good night's sleep, to sleep as soundly as a lion. And to snore so much as to rouse the blessed wrath of the neighbors. And. Or I need a drink. To keep drinking until I fall asleep, no growl, no thoughts. But drinking cloys. Life palls. I would like to redecorate the interior of my soul. To wake up with the sun on my face. To feel alive. Alive. And.

Better get off this kick or you'll go nuts. Three hours and fifty minutes to go. I don't feel like doing anything, not a thing. I don't want to sit down or stand up or read or fall asleep or wake up or flirt with anyone or pick a fight. Try the balcony.

The cold does you good. It wakes you up. But then, you don't know what to do with yourself once awake. Let's mosey over to the bar. The bar is empty and I get sick just looking at a glass. Dante. Nice but stupid. He doesn't like me. Well, neither do I. The eatery: let's eat. Eat plastic? We can't. Damn.

Three hours and thirty minutes to go.

"Wake me at seven, will you? Thanks."

I lie down and doze off on a bench. Outside voices mingle with inner voices. Memories gallop in herds, I see senseless pictures. A nameless corner, that filthy lavatory door that opens onto Chicago, faces seen, faces remembered, agitated faces always hurriedly babbling a foreign language, faces, unplaced faces: where was it, when was it, how was it, what for? Coughing. Twelve hours without coughing, I am surprised. It wakes me up a bit, but I fall back into a drowsy haze of clouds, voices, highways, planes, drinks, dark rooms of distant hotels, books, classrooms, notebooks, purses, signs, notes, the hot sidewalks of the city in summer, dreamy beautiful women who stalk like tigers, x-ray plates, vials, injections, bathtubs, coughing . . .

Sleep now.

■■■ 35

Every two weeks, my wife says: I hope you're not writing another word against this regime.

She says: Remember what happened to you.

What we went through.

I think, on account of one sentence: "The true . . .", etc.

I look at her, keep quiet, write, and do not publish anything.

I wait.

Alone.

In the shadows with my typewriter, a folding table, a stack of paper, and a bottle, I write:

"To freedom, even if it lasts only fifteen minutes."

Me.

Alone.

▪▪▪ 36

Anarchist? Madman? Communist? Radical?

I accept it; I used to fear being accused of these things.

Or even one of them. Or one at a time, each in turn, and from week to week.

Now: Pshaw!

Somebody among friends: He's crazy.

Somebody else, among friends: He's a Communist!

Somebody else, among friends: He's a radical!

Somebody else, among friends: The reactionaries silenced him.

Me: Pshaw!

You, with your hand on your heart: But . . . what do I care about left-wingers and right-wingers? I want to live in peace!

And you read the comic strips.

Ah, but . . . with a certain severity:

What about the truth?

The truth.

Of course, we have a few Quixotes of the truth.

A THOUSAND DAYS:

"If people bring so much courage to this world the world has to kill them to break them, so of course it kills them. The world breaks everyone and afterward many are strong at the broken places. But those that will not break it kills. It kills the very good and the very gentle and the very brave impartially."

So said Don Ernest, and Schlessinger the Kid quoted him.

Dallas.

Thank you, Art.

"I have plowed the sea."

Thank you, Don Simón.

"I only ask the nation for another reward."

Much obliged, Marshal Sucre.

"E pur si muove!"

Grazie, Don Galo.

"Verily, I say unto you . . ." But.

Is it necessary to continue?

Truth is a commitment to cyanide.

It is fire, a dagger, an assassin's bullet, a cross.

But to those of us who cannot serve the lie . . . we who cannot be the Beast, we who consent to be robbed without raising our fists . . . who want to while away afternoons patting little heads and playing pinochle—what chances are left for us?

To those of us who say, If I speak the truth, it is not my neck, it's my little ones' . . . And if I don't speak the truth, I lose my taste for living. The meaning of my life, etc., etc.

What refuge does truth leave us?

Eat it and shut up.

Pay up and shut up.

Take it and shut up.

Shut up.

And don't just shut up: pretend to be satisfied.

Shout: *Viva! Viva!*

Declare: We never had it better.

Affirm: No one is dying of hunger.

Report: Progress is progressing.

Insist: How well everything is going!

Exclaim: I like the Pile of Shit!

And bequeath it to your children.

For those of us who cannot be the Beast, the only thing left to live on is lying.

Living with the lie.

Living off the lie, for the lie . . .

You cannot. Cannibal, you cannot.

Cain, you cannot.

Then you must die.

Then you must publish. Again!

To be a leper, again:

"Coward, you're only keeping quiet because you were in jail."

"Old geezer, now you won't write any stupid lies."

"Idiot, what do you care? Who do you think you are, Christ?"

"Ha! They finally shut you up. You viper!"

"Radical!"

Natalia: Right now, when we're starting to save?

And them: Daddy . . . where's Daddy?

Somebody else: Yes, of course . . . but.

The Beast: Come over here!

And me: It's that . . . life tasted of ashes. The days smelled of death . . . bitterness in my mouth forever . . . Why be a chrysalis if you will never become a butterfly? I . . . only wanted . . . I'm sorry: I never dreamt that I was so dangerous . . . I want to live . . . But to feel like I'm alive, not dead . . .

Voices and echoes: But . . . It would have been so simple . . . so easy to live with the lie!

"The lie is beautiful. It is good: it protects you against the Beast. Not only does it protect you against the Beast, it makes the Beast work for you."

"And it shall make you prosper."

"It will take you to the mountaintop and show you the world."

"Follow me," it will say, "and all this will be yours." And you serve it and, yes, it shall be yours.

People will not stare at you with hate; they will never shout:

"That one, that one there, he hears the song: disembowel him!"

Heads will bow to you. An inexhaustible panoply of honors will unfold before you. Medals will hang from your starched shirt. Flowers will adorn your grave. Your likeness will be sculpted in stone. And you will look better than you actually look.

Your pockets will be filled with gold. All you can grab.

Posterity, if such a thing still exists, will honor you.

The lie is beautiful, it is generous.

It does not promise other, uncertain worlds of pleasure to come.

It works well, in cash. Here and now.

Just when you need it.

▪▪▪ 37

It would seem that a simple error in education is what sparks a desire to serve the truth.

The child must resolve . . .

Parents who teach their children to love truth and despise falsehood sentence them to a life of grief, disappointment, tragedy and poverty, inhuman misery.

Only a few of these children say later: "I am what I am despite my education, not because of it." They learn that their parents were mistaken. The rest harbor a love of truth, a need for truth, a nebulous, undefined but heartfelt, intuitive truth, just as a dog harbors an instinct to bay at the moon.

They cannot explain this love. Sometimes they regret this need.

Sometimes they curse it. In their search for this truth, when they dare to draw too near it, they pay a price in flesh and blood.

They and their kinsmen.

All because their parents brought them up in a certain

way and impressed certain basic ideas upon them before they learned to reason for themselves.

It is like the poison of reading—you learn to read before you learn of its risks. Later, we suffer its delights and we pursue them for life, though they lead us to the brink.

It is like the fury that makes lemmings hurl themselves into the sea.

Makes Daniels enter the lion's den.

It is like having an ugly face.

You are born with a face and you have to walk with it every day, day after day, until the end of your days. And you do not decide one fine day to get rid of your face, because you do not want to miss the adventure of being alive.

So you live, tolerating your face.

A few people call this heroism.

Others, stupidity.

So many call it stupidity that there is no more heroism. No more Joans of Arc, no more Quixotes, no more Peters.

It is all stupidity in the end: black is white.

Tomorrow, when one of the arbiters of white and black decides he wants to amuse himself with a stupid war, he will send his Beasts to my house and demand my blood. And my children's.

If I refuse, he will help himself to my blood. And my children's.

He will have me called a traitor.

He will revile my name.

He, who once embraced our enemies. He, who needed to find a way to fool his subjects. He, who learned to serve the lie and used its gold to buy the Beast. And I, who did not serve him, who asked him for nothing but a bit of sun—move back, don't block the light, let me earn my living—I will be forgotten in ignominy.

Tonight I can do nothing but write.

Like a mule walking in circles around a windmill. Like a donkey who eyes the carrot. No, worse. Because I know I am a donkey chasing his carrot.

For I know I shall never reach it.

For I know that I am alone.

Alone, between three children and two cells.

Alone, bound by the chains the Beast and Love have woven around me.

Alone in the night, writing and chasing an unreachable carrot because I know very well it is all I can do.

This is also a humble kind of heroism; with a small "h."

■■■ 38

To backstitch, then:

Flaco: You're not working anymore because you have nothing to tell . . .

Me: But . . . I do.

Flaco: Ha! After twelve years of bourgeois life, marriage and the whole routine, what could you possibly have to tell?

Me: Ana's story.

Flaco: How does it go?

Me: Ana Anita's story.

Flaco: Tell it, tell it . . .

Me: Once upon a time . . .

Flaco: I'll treat you to coffee.

■■■ 39

Camels.

Needles.

If I hadn't heard that fable I'd never . . .

No.

Don't deny your refusals.
Don't open your mind to the Beast's seething slime.
Good night.
Tomorrow, perhaps, the sun will rise on the other side.
And two plus two will equal five.
Hunger will be satisfied.
Justice will be done.
God will be on the phone.
And he won't be deaf anymore.
It will be like the song.
Perhaps.

■■■ 40

It was a Sunday in August and we went hang gliding.
My wife said: No, it's dangerous.
My children, all three: Don't go, Daddy, don't go.
And I said: I'm going.
Hero.
I went.
Ayar Huchu. Golden Eagle.
We flew all afternoon over the frozen sea, over the highland I love.
And over our inland sea, Titicaca, frozen and blue.
With the clouds and the wind.
The instructor said: Do you feel the hot air on your back?
Go up!
And I push the lever up.
And I went up.
And came down. And softly soared.
Four hours.
Metal bird, whispering river of wind. Flap, flap, flap, the wings.

The sun was going down in an explosion of red when we finally touched down, black little worms now if seen from above.

Natalia: . . . you don't remember that you have commitments . . . duties, responsibilities. You only think of yourself . . . of yourself, and yourself alone . . .

Them: Was it pretty, up there?

Me: O swallow, swallow . . .

Ayar Huchu.

I flew that day.

Was I happy.

FOUR

It is raining outside.

I remember the words of the judges in La Paz who dismissed my third novel: "This is too personal a story."

Zaz! They wrung its neck. I never managed to win a prize. Oh well.

If I ever see these words in print, I can imagine what those judges will say.

"It is so personal a story, not literary enough."

Not serious enough.

To write this way, I suppose the author must have very little respect for his readers. What madness, to do one's dirty laundry in public as if it mattered in the least!

It is raining outside. I have given up my lunch hour to sit here alone in the office. I should be writing to my creditors to request a one-week extension. Why am I wasting time with this piece of paper?

I put my hand to my heart and ask, "Why are you doing this?"

I answer: To know what it means to be what I am. To find out who I am, to tell my family—and my Family—what my House is like, what my home is like, what our executioners are like, what it means to be born here, to be alive and present, to be searching for a way out of this labyrinth.

After all, I console myself, I am starting to take a shine to what comes out of my typewriter.

This could even prove useful to someone. I mean, after I use it for a while to keep chasing my carrot, I prompt myself.

Since the best do not do it, it must be me, in my humble humility, who must attempt to uncover the essential nooks of our identity. I get ready for takeoff.

Also, because they are somehow guilty too—they, my family and my Family—for what is going on, I am almost airborne.

I take off: because I need to. And I fly: because I want to. That is why I do this. There is no better reason.

Come what may, and God bless me.

For those faceless brothers of my Death Row Clan. For those who go on and on and on.

Those who will, perhaps, change things. For those who will make the song sweeter. More optimistic.

Those who will follow. That's why. That's who.

That's why this one will not go hunting after prizes, will never have colored dust jackets. If it is ever printed, I will have to foot the bill. And then try and sell it.

But, to begin with, because even the deaf scream in search of an echo.

An echo of an echo of an echo of an echo.

▪▪▪ 42

Peru under Prado. The strike at.
He was a young officer . . .
Bah.

▪▪▪ 43

Natalia: "What are you doing? Come to bed."
"In a minute."

Love, then, has chains. Today is Friday and I am not drinking.

I have given to Caesar what is Caesar's. These stolen hours are mine: I have paid for this time. I like these shapes, I just love the "Q."

Natalia: "Come to bed."

"In a moment."

By day it is Caesar; by night, Love. The stolen hours are for chasing my carrot.

Yesterday, Flaco: "Write, man, write!"

Julio: "Minutiae . . ."

Me.

Alone.

■■■ 44

Peru under Prado. The strike at.

He was a young officer standing on a painted white line in the street.

The miners surged forward, children first, women behind them, men bringing up the rear. The flag of the fatherland.

Their fatherland.

My fatherland.

We were standing on the narrow sidewalk. We warmed our hands with our breath. Clouds grazed the big mountain. Day was just breaking. Unconcerned, the gray sun blinked.

He said:

"I'll kill the first one to step over this line."

And he retreated thirty paces.

Nothing happened.

We went into a dark stall. Calendars with Vargas girls. Portable stoves. Condensed milk. A cup of coffee to keep the cold away.

Some, motionless there, with the flag. Eyes hoping for a miracle, silently.

Others here, scratching their armpits, a finger in the nose. Looking out for rats from the sewers. Hugging the barrel of their rifles. Squatting and watching the streets. Click!—a trigger. Don't look, don't even look, brothers.

"Nothing is going to happen," someone says.

Can you imagine, they come forward. Dragging their feet along the cobblestones. Silently looking far away, at their own death.

We went outside. I took pictures, waited.

The girl crossed the line, the officer raised the gun, nestled it fondly in the hollow of his hand, and fired.

The girl died.

An uproar ensued. Running, shouting, screeching, cursing, barking. Bullets. Swords. Strong horses of the Cavalry.

Silence. A long silence afterward, and then moaning.

Notice how I tell it. Observe how it is nearly devoid of propaganda. Admire my manner, acting as if nothing happened. Qualify how offhandedly I tender the story.

Don't anyone else call me a radical again.

After all, the girl was a Peruvian. A foreigner. Her death could not have hurt as much as it would have hurt a Bolivian girl, right? Right? She died far away, didn't she? It is not as if this had happened in Catavi. Or in Siglo XX. Not near here, not one of us. It's not the same, is it? No. It is not. It is not.

Yet I remember her face as if I saw it yesterday. Though it happened in Peru under Prado. And I remember the officer as if I'd seen him today. The military under Prado. I remember her blood as if it were mine, though it was Prado's blood.

Maybe—just maybe, I say—the girl died only for me to tell the story seventeen years later like I do today, laying it before you as if I couldn't care less.

Worse yet would be not even to lay it before you in this manner.

It would be as if the girl had never been born.

Or had never died. As if she had never been.

And neither had I.

■■■ 45

It must seem that by now I have accurately identified my enemies.

I have not.

I cannot consider them my enemies, because I know they are hungry and ignorant. I do not hold them responsible for their actions.

It's those words. "Forgive them, for they know not . . ."

I cannot even say that I admit the Beast is my enemy.

No, not after my acquaintance with the Beast. After five days and two cells, I cannot call him my enemy because I am afraid I too may be like the Beast.

But I do not want to be the Lamb.

Up close, the Beast inspires pity. He is only a beast. And his eyes, always faltering, do not let you hate him thoroughly, hate him enough to tear him limb from limb. You cannot hate an opossum. Or a hyena.

This is my strength. And my weakness. This feeling of intellectual superiority that grants him a position of physical superiority.

I am superior, so I cannot kill him. He is superior, so he can kill me. Or have me killed.

I wish his bullets were blank.

Like mine: I have nothing but words.

But I cannot let myself identify with the Beast. I would despise myself forever.

I will never do what he does, nor can he ever do what I do, what I am able to do.

For as long as I believe that, the best will remember me. This is my strength. My superiority.

The Beast's strength is not knowing the first thing about any of this, not aspiring to live in anyone's memory, not knowing the day he was born, and believing he will never perish.

Consequently, I am lost.

And so are they. It is my strength and my weakness to know that I am lost. Their strength and their weakness, never to have wondered or wanted to know. They are too busy keeping from dying of hunger. They kill because they want to eat. Simple.

Someone should lay a bridge between the girl from Peru and the Beast.

When I remember that the last time anyone tried was two thousand years ago, and when I see what I see, my hair stands on end.

And in my anguish, I look for and listen to the siren song.

For, and I must say this, sometimes I think the song does not exist. I have invented it so that I can step into my shoes, fill up my days, look at the world and be able to bear it.

Sometimes I think I invented this carrot.

But most of the time, I still hear the song.

▪ ▪ ▪ 46

In Oruro, a college student who was the salt of the earth, silly as an angel, got up and said, as if addressing Christ's older brother:

"As an avant-garde writer, can you offer a simple formula to cure our country's ills over the next ten years?"

"One hundred and eighty Presidents have been trying, for a hundred and fifty years. They have killed people, starved people, murdered people, and they also have served people. You, a rearguard college student, are asking me for a formula that is nowhere to be found."

With wet eyes and a transparent heart, the man asked:

"And how will we fight Brazil, when it invades?"

The first question was impossible. But there was a way out of the second: "How many people live in Brazil?"

"I don't know," the good man said honestly.

"How many people live in Bolivia?"

"Six million," he answered, puffing out his chest. That was before the census.

"Brazil has over ninety-six million. If they invade, each one of us will have to kill an average of sixteen Brazilians. That is, if none of us get killed."

Frowning, he swallowed and became pensive.

I finished him:

"As someone once said, 'we will return to the sea in Brazilian tanks.'"

I did not say that mistakes exact a price, that stupidity costs money, land, and blood, because I had truly tired of saying such things.

Also because, as any well-dressed patriot with a gray suit, a startling necktie, a desk, and a nice office knows, to say such things is to betray our country, isn't it?

Saying such things is treason; hence, we are lost.

By not saying them, we sentence our country to death. It's that simple.

So-called avant-garde journalists—poor innocent student!—go to jail if we say these things. The perpetual wise guys who never say them get to the presidential palace and even have statues erected in their honor.

Statues later honored with bird spots by divine justice. Honors never granted to our graves, usually anonymous and unmarked.

There is a pro and a con to everything.

But to whom do you tell these things?

When it comes to saying things, the first blunder is

when you have said something in all honesty and sincerity and then lean out the window and eagerly wait for an echo.

The echo:

When it comes to saying things, the second blunder is when you come down from the balcony and walk among people and repeat the things you said and wait, still eagerly, for an echo.

The echo:

When it comes to saying things, the next blunder is when, out in the open, you say to them again, directly addressing the very people who ought to be listening, aiming your words like bullets, and then prick up your ears and still somewhat eagerly wait for an echo.

The echo:

The last blunder, hardest of all to recognize and accept, is perpetrated a lifetime later when, nearly out of breath, you speak the same words, you prick up your ears still a trifle eagerly, and wait for an echo.

The echo:

■■■ 47

There are other blunders: rich men are always bad; poor men, always good. The humble are always worthy, the powerful always sleazy. The penniless will inherit the heavens, the well-dressed will go to hell.

It's a rough trap to fall into because it can last a hundred years. Two lifetimes. You fall into it when you believe that just because a man is less well-off—because he has very limited means, means so meager there's nothing left to see—he is a better man.

The humble masses who deserve my sacrifice. My head.

The good, kind masses who explain and justify my demise.

The suffering masses who clamor for my blood.

And my children's.

The masses, those teeming masses whose steps will make the earth tremble when the day of the great words dawns.

The average intelligent person can waste twenty years believing this fable. And he can chastise himself for the masses until he achieves a second-rate martyrology.

But, when all is said and done:

Napoleon: "History is written with the blood of the masses."

Stalin: "The death of thirty-five million buys hope for two hundred and sixty million."

The masses.

Perhaps you need to live for a long time before you learn the axiom:

For the masses, to the masses, without the masses.

From this blunder several platitudes follow.

The most common one: every ruler gets the masses he deserves.

Ergo: every mass has the ruler it deserves.

And the scribblers it deserves.

Some rulers get hanged, most scribblers get shunted aside.

Fair is fair.

Death by asphyxia lasts three minutes. Books dream in libraries for thirty years. Masses languish for thirty centuries.

If suffering and agony are what it's all about, make mine short. It hurts.

Very fair.

Hanged men, ignored men, men in eternal agony: such is the price of our blunders and false carrots.

The blind hordes of History . . .

Who has not walked along these streets, shouldering his misfortune, limping like a dog with a broken paw?

The great blunder: the masses believe everything is

done for them, whereas individuals never work for the masses.

Great men don't, nor do the humble, the powerful, or the composers.

The masses are the pretext for every person to pursue his particular carrot.

For the chrysalis to become a butterfly.

The lieutenant to become President.

The scribbler to backstitch his syllables.

"Homo ludicus."

Ludic man.

Ludic masses.

Everything must change so that things remain the same.

But what matters is to try and understand this sublime game.

They say.

■ ■ ■ 48

Then it is four in the morning and I am backstitching nonsense when I hear on the door: knock, knock, knock.

In this country you can only expect the worst if it is four in the morning and you hear a knock, knock, knock on your door.

The police, I tell myself. What have I done now, what did I write?

The door: knock, knock, knock.

A mournful sound. Like the Ninth.

I hesitate. I sweat. I tremble. I wish it were a thief, I think to myself.

But the gentle rapping continues, insistent: knock, knock, knock.

Then: Thy will be done, I say, and open the door a crack.

There he is, exhausted. Worn thin by the centuries of centuries. But it's him.

The same parted beard. The same hair, golden and shoulder-length. The same white tunic, under the moon-light. The same eyes: penetrating, kind, sad. The same bare feet.

I shout like my grandmother used to shout, frightened by a ghost.

"Jesus!"

He does not speak. He just looks at me, asking for something. A demand. An entreaty.

"Lord!", I say, fearfully.

He says nothing. There he is, standing in the doorway, because history and man's memory are mistaken: they invented Judas, but there never was a Judas.

"Master!", I say hoarsely.

His eyes grip me. I hesitate. But no, I could not do it, never. Me? Never. I cannot.

"Christ . . . ," I whisper.

But he already knows. He turns and goes to the house next door.

I hear on the door, far away: knock, knock, knock.

They made a mistake, I want to scream. A mistake that lasted twenty centuries, I think, amazed. Do something, do something, I demand.

But the street is empty. The moon paints everything white and the white shadow is already lost in the white street.

It cannot be, I tell myself. I am very tired, I reason. But he was there. I wonder. You are overworked, I try telling myself.

But, while smoking a cigarette, I wonder: it is impossible. Then I know.

For the first time, the masses did not do what they must do. That's impossible, I state now.

Every man is entitled to his song.

The masses have never failed to play their role.

They have always provided the best of pretexts.

▪▪▪ 49

But then, Donne:

"No man is an island."

Oh, I agree. Without a doubt. I need them. I die a little with each death. I mourn with each moan. My eyes mist over in pain for all that should be but isn't, for the song. I do what I can and contribute my tithe.

Ludic man.

It is the story of Hans Schmidt.

Schmidt, the man who did astrological charts.

Hansie, who made up the chart for the Weimar Republic.

And for the Führer.

Both charts, in the end, for the German masses.

When all seemed lost for the German masses, Goebbels read it to Hitler. In the Chancellery bunker in Berlin, two days before Herr Adolf's death, and while the Russians battled the Volkstrum—old men and children, the German masses—for control of every stone and alley:

"A fantastic fact has come to light, for both horoscopes show the war beginning in 1939. The victories lasting through 1941, the subsequent series of reversals, with the hardest blows coming during the first months of 1945, particularly during the first half of April.

"In the second half of April we were to experience a temporary success. Then there would be stagnation until August and peace that same month. For the following three years Germany would have a hard time, but starting in 1948 she would rise again."

Then: Marshall.

For not only do Saviors find in the masses their reason to be; so do the masters of the Beast. Fine: by 1950, the Germans could not believe what their Führer had done. By 1960 they swore that Fritz was a mere legend. By 1970 the German mark was almost on par with the dollar. By 1980 it will be stronger than the dollar.

By 1990 the Führer will be like the wicked witch: a name invoked to scare little children who will not go to bed.

The masses are eternal. No need to worry about them.

The problem is not the Son of Man.

It is the son of man.

The talking biped, that's who.

He who lives across the street from my house. He who hesitates. He who has children, debts, dreams, ambitions, fears.

He who makes the world turn.

The orphan who can never call out:

"Father, why hast Thou forsaken me?"

That's who.

■■■ 50

If the son of man is an image between two parallel mirrors, why should he suffer so much?

Why should he chase a shoreline and never reach it?

Why should he have to imagine a star that he knows does not exist?

Why do we believe that two plus two equals five; why do we need it to be thus, when two plus two will always, eternally, equal four?

Why is it that the song cannot be silenced?

FIVE

▪▪▪ 51

Brothers and Sisters, we are like the dog that is forever turning around and around, chasing his tail.

And this agony endures, it endures still, as the poet wrote. What it is in the sky, so it is in a drop of water.

So yes, here I am, forever turning around and around, chasing my tail.

And yes, here we are all, eternally chasing our collective tail.

And it endures, yes, this agony endures still.

This is how it was when he was born in 1912, turned up at El Chaco, returned with a piece of lead in his chest, walked alone into church one day, came out in tandem, saw that we were on the way, guessed what we would turn out to be when he saw us, wanted to believe that two plus two equals five, did what had to be done but failed because in spite of doing what had to be done, he failed, and he is eternally turning around in me, in the others, biting his tail.

This was how I started turning around too, staying around even when I thought I was leaving, trying to understand the turns, the tail, the reason for turning and returning, saying what had been said, trying to say more, seeing how those who came after me had come, smiling his slightly sad smile, wanting to believe that two plus two equals five and, this is how I know it, eternally turning around and around in the others, biting my tail.

This is how I see those who came after me, so little, wondering: "Tell us, where was the sea they took from us . . . ?", reading the books I read, singing the songs I sang, thinking what I thought, feeling happy under the wind of the *puna* when the sun shines on the lake, eating what I ate, breathing what I breathed, sensing something wrong in the stories their elders tell, alleged stories, false stories, authentic, honest stories, feeling, as I say, a breach, a cleavage, a rupture, something that hurts, something that is wrong and can never be righted, something that is to be the same thing . . . this is how I see them and this is how they stand there, so little, so small, turning and turning around themselves, alone, eternally chasing their tail in the others because what they feel and see and hear does not fulfill their hearts, no. It is not enough, not persuasive, it cannot be but it is, and it hurts.

And those who talk to me—the man who wrote twenty-six books, the one who memorized the great tragedy day by day, hour by hour (blow by blow); the man who can recount it all, betrayal by betrayal, the man who won the pointless debate in Quito and even the man who believed that blood was the only way out of this blind alley and so he bathed in blood . . . in the end, they are all turning around themselves, chasing our never-ending tail, looking at others as I look at them and as they look at me, half-sadly, half-angrily, with enmity, resentment; orphans, naked orphans who know that for us the hour has not struck, will and cannot strike, and we ourselves have muted the bell; guilty and yet able—more than able—to keep chasing our tails, holding our heads high, saying a thing or three, feeling the breach, the rapture, the tragedy, and still going on, time after time, chasing the same collective tail in the same place, with the same doubts, in the same sadness, following the same trail we inherited, in the same long agony, so cruel, so senseless, that will be all we bequeath as it was all we inherited.

Some fraternal ties are as heavy as God's wrath.

▪ ▪ ▪ 52

This is what unites us: failure.

The tireless chasing of our collective tail.

The ability to keep turning, nailed to the same doubt, century after century .

The ability to smile every day at dusk and to look into our children's eyes as we improvise a look as pure as theirs.

Our tradition of inventing gestures, songs, and words, and to rest afterwards and even to sleep peacefully, as if we were truly tired.

The will to accept, nearly without shame, this enduring agony that endures and endures still.

The complicity.

Because, in which turn did we murder honesty?

In which twist did we decide, once and for all, to leave behind nothing more than this?

When did it happen that we accepted the idea of condemning ourselves to turn around and around, to ask, to forget, and to deny?

In which dark hour did we decide, all of us, not to draw the sword, except to destroy ourselves?

When, in which twist, did we will the agony to last forever and ever, postponing until never our moment of truth?

When shall we cease to fight among ourselves and begin to fight for ourselves?

When shall the great wound heal, when shall it be

sealed and the scar become nearly invisible? When shall we, through with spinning, begin to walk, and take our place in the sun?

When will we be able to look each other in the eye without being so very frightened of the shame we share, so that it will no longer be necessary to keep spinning?

When will we decide that the time has come to cure, once and for all, this keen pain, our perpetual anguish, our plodding steps, the blame we have always shunned, in order to truly grow weary, so that we can rest at last and leave a clear horizon to those who will follow?

When did we deny the time to leave, to leave once and for all, cutting through the time with a single stroke, to leave behind this grave doubt?

When will we begin to be, instead of just pretending to be?

When will this sordid mockery end, this daily mockery, mockery that we inflict and suffer, mockery that passes and falls from father to son, infinite mockery, mockery that seals our fate?

When will we rediscover pride?

When will we learn to respect the generations to come?

When will a child be able to tell his child a story different from the one he heard from his father?

When will the hour of heroism arrive? When?

Oh, how bitter it can be, being sentenced to listen to the song.

▪▪▪ 53

And nevertheless, in my lifetime I did not find a single guilty soul.

When I came to be, already with phantom limbs, I had to answer my son's question: " . . . Where was our sea . . . ?" by saying the usual thing, doing the usual thing, telling the same thing others tell, and I was not guilty. I said what others had said and written and shouted in city squares and villages, what others had rhymed and composed and sung, hummed and explained, and we all did what we did without ever feeling guilty.

This is the heart of our tragedy.

We are all innocent.

We all do what we do, did what we did, and will even do what we will do in order to live in good conscience, in order to relieve ever so slightly the very solitary torment that endures and endures still.

What a paradox, to all be innocent and to find ourselves guilty.

What a fate, ours, to all feel that we are carrying within ourselves such a deep, inevitable, stinging wound and to know ourselves to be innocent.

What men we are, we who can lay down our lives to destroy the paradox, alter our fate, we who can die, and even live on, plowing the sea.

How exceptional we are, for in a world of self-preserving creatures, we are very efficient at the continuous task of destroying ourselves.

What certainty we possess, knowing we all are wise and finding we have all been mistaken.

What vision we possess, we who see such a clear truth, but can so easily pursue a mirage.

And what loneliness we inhabit, the solitude of one who never agrees with himself.

Thus we endure, turning circles in our innocence, never able to look at our own foes, but with only one consolation: the individual passes on, but the species does not: for the individual, no misfortune can last a hundred years.

Our innocence is, in truth, monstrous.

It has rendered nearly every sacrifice senseless.

It has weakened nearly every ideal.

It has heightened nearly every excess.

It has converted the valley of God into a wasteland of sadness.

And it leaves everything balanced where nothing is dramatic . . . or comic or serious or trivial or noble or evil.

We are, we affirm, but we are not.

This complicity.

But I insist: I still hear it.

▪▪▪ 54

And I quote because . . . am I perchance after a literary prize?

I quote:

". . . Poor sections can be found in every city in the world, but our miners' misery has its own ambiance: wrapped in cold and constant wind; curiously, it ignores man. It is colorless, nature is dressed in gray. The ore, which has contaminated the earth's core, has made it barren. Four to five thousand meters up, where nothing grows, not even rough straw, sits the miners' camp.

"The mountain, angered by man, wants to be rid of him. The water flowing out of the mineralized core is poisonous. Inside the galleries, a yellow, foul-smelling liquid called copaquira drips continuously, burning holes in the miners' clothing.

"Hundreds of kilometers away, rivers and fish die after absorbing the liquid poison the machines eject. The ore is extracted and converted, but the soil becomes polluted. Wealth is transformed into poverty. And there, in that cold, seeking protection in the bosom of the mountain where grain dares not venture, we find the miners.

"Camps lined up symmetrically like prison blocks, crude huts with stone and mud walls that are covered with old newspapers; zinc roofs and dirt floors; the wind blowing from the pampa penetrates the cracks and if the family, huddled together in make-shift beds—usually, a few pelts—does not freeze, it runs the risk of suffocating.

"Ensconced behind these walls live hungry people with weak lungs who work in three *puntas* around the clock, the 'veinticuatreo.'

"(In the big mines, work is carried out in three shifts of *puntas*. The 'veinticuatreo' is a twenty-four-hour shift inside the mine. Day laborers usually are contracted to perform this work, or jobbers hire other workers to do it. The *maquipura,* or temporary worker, is a pariah: he has no rights and is a direct descendant of the *mitayos* or *mingados** from colonial times. At the present time, thousands of *maquipuras* work in the nationalized mining industry.)

"There is no past or future here, just overwhelming misery. The camp, tucked into some corner, just sits there: beyond lies loneliness; within, poverty.

"The inhabitants of this sordid eternity are reminiscent of the condemned of Czarist villages, because they are equally segregated, suffering an indefinite sentence. This is the miners' exile."

▪▪▪ 55

This man was Sergio Almaraz. No one killed him. He killed himself, legally: ulcers. He was not a suicide. A suicide he was not. But neither was his death natural. How could it be, at forty? To die at forty is almost a crime. But living forty years without dignity is a crime. Hence: ulcers. Almaraz is innocent: he was not an accomplice, he is a witness.

---

*Indians paid for public or forced labor

How I miss him now, my friend Almaraz: I never knew him, but how I miss him. As much as I miss Cesar Vallejo.

But I, I am alone.

▪▪▪ 56

I would like to be able to hate those who want to kill me, those who will kill me if they can, because they believe that I am their enemy.

I would like to cease believing in my friends, the lunatics who taught me that two plus two equals five, that a person can be happy, that one must love one's neighbor, that one cannot go to sleep without reading a good paragraph, my friends whose sorrows gave me insomnia, but I cannot stop believing in my friends. I cannot and will not.

I would like to feel as others do, who hate. I would like to hate the one who harasses me.

I cannot.

Sometimes, I want to hate them, but I cannot.

Maybe, just maybe, private scorn.

But that is all.

Such is man.

So kill me.

I cannot. My imagination hurtles me into the Beast's brain. It makes me think like the Beast. Makes me be one.

And allows me to find excuses as the Beast does. I am innocent, like the Beast: predating sin.

Oh, damn it . . . the Beast is going to murder me and I cannot hate them.

This song echoes horribly in my head.

And to wonder that it all began when I learned how to read.

It was a sunny afternoon.

I was a child.

I still am, that's it.

The Beast marches on.

And wins.

Never to learn to share others' contempt for corpses.

To be here, hating the whole business and suffering for the anonymous dead.

Why read, then?

Why can't I fall asleep, finally?

Finally.

Pleasant perfume of the last bend in the road.

Finally.

Pretty word.

Yes.

But no: the road has not ended.

The final footprint has not yet been left.

Chesterton: "The tragedy is that things seem logical and are not."

That is the mistake.

Thinking that things are logical.

Trying to make sense of them. Believing there is a reason to be.

Thinking about the one who is judging.

We inherited weakness.

And our reward lies in the beyond.

Not that it is true; it's that we cannot believe otherwise.

Otherwise than . . .

All together now:

The siren song.

Now, curtains.

▪▪▪ 57

In the freezing night, the moon shines almost like the sun.

And the closed flowers sigh.

My Brothers and Sisters sleep, innocently.

Suns of other universes shine, ten thousand more stars here than on any other peak.

The eyes of my city blink, reflection of the sky.

Standing by the window, I smoke and shiver.

I look at my children, traveling through dreamland.

A cat crosses the garden.

A dog barks in the distance.

A rooster.

This sky of mine, transparent and frozen, the mountains on the moon look—how do they say—as if they were right down here.

I smoke, look out the window, and listen to my children breathe.

I am happy.

This is my country, I tell myself, as the snow on this mountain of mine twinkles in eternity.

I would never, ever want to be someone else.

How foolish I am, I think. What is the matter with me? Nothing, man.

You love this country.

That's all it is.

What else could it be?

▪▪▪ 58

Nivolize?

Let's nivolize:

My "Communism" was a product of Belaunde's gonads, observed and reported by *Stern* and the Chinese dailies of Lima, whose Cantonese pro-Communist propaganda was always Chinese to me, although Wilkinson would say otherwise; ask her, she is in Montevideo now.

In six hours, the Peruvians and the British were in perfect agreement as to my irrefutable "Communism."

A discreet, courteous note advised me that I was fired. A categorical and dry order saw to it that no one, not a soul in the entire Viceroyalty, would hire the quarrelsome Communist. In two pen strokes they sentenced me to starvation.

My hunger lasted for ten thousand, eight hundred hours.

A very annoying hunger. Like a leech in your gut.

Like your gums smelling of rot, of dry desperation.

I did not notice at first. The severance pay coming to me when I was fired with a smile amounted to a small fortune.

And when you are relatively young, you are overly optimistic. I never dreamed that blacklists actually existed.

Who would think that. Etc.

So I spent all my money on Mother and little Egghead.

We had a swell time that summer in Huampani.

When they left for La Paz, I was out on the street, or one step short of being there.

As months melted away, so did people and things.

A nice apartment on the twenty-first floor. My good green and blue suits. My fashionable ties. My fine shoes. My not-so-fine shoes. My records. My bicycle, which I used to ride to keep trim. My entire hi-fi system. My portable radio. My blankets.

My friends.

Everything but my books.

One day, in a two-by-two hole-in-the-wall, I found myself with a pile of books, a mattress, a pair of blue jeans, and a green shirt.

The hole had one of those little windows, you know, like in restaurants; a little wooden window is sent up and on the ledge is a plate of food.

I spent fifty hundred and forty hours in there.

I only went out at night. I walked over to the park, looked at the gray sea from the garbage-strewn cliff, smoked, thought, strolled.

During the day some friends would come by to commission translations, which they paid for with worn bills. I exchanged the bills for food, purchased at street corner stands. Or for Sublime Chocolate bars. Or for black tobacco Inca cigarettes.

It was there that I discovered white hairs were growing in my once rather reddish beard. That fleas became a terrible affliction. That without noticing it, you can start talking to yourself out loud. It was there that I wrote another bad novel: working title, *Sand*.

I found that, in the gray world of Lima, fine ocean sand gets into everything. Drinking glasses, head, beard, typewriter, mattress. With a dash of magic realism, as they call it nowadays, it was easy for this black dust, wind-crushed pieces of seashells, to invade hearts, souls, pockets, cathedrals, children.

When the sand of my novel reached my neck, I stopped writing because I did not want to suffocate.

I mean, go crazy.

I did not go crazy. At least, not officially.

Because the owners of my hole-in-the-wall threw me out.

Friends could no longer find me. I left my books at a friend's house and began to roam the streets.

I roamed in the shadows with my blue jeans, tufts of long hair, a green shirt, and a bundle of typewritten scrap paper, legal size, from the office. I roamed for three days.

All was lost, save the song.

■ ■ ■ 59

Seven years later, and with that bundle of paper transformed into printed matter with a two-color cover and all, I received a gold ornament from the mayor of La Paz that made me believe I was the Hemingway of the Choqueyapu.

Nine thousand copies of my scrap papers, legal size, were sold.

I got stuck inside that bundle of scrap paper, legal size, and there I shall remain forever, a desperate and cynical adolescent.

Never again will I be that kid who believed that life was a glass of milk and went out into the world to see for whom the bell tolls.

More griped than blissful now I spend my days on these sleepy streets, sunk in a deadly routine, and falling prey to the greatest frustration, that of having been sentenced to never harvest any echo.

When I cannot avoid it, I look in the mirror and find right there, among those commas and tildes, an unspeakable desire: because I will live forever in that kid, and since I managed to breathe some life into him, the idea of leaving behind this vale of tears at this very moment should not be so bad, after all.

Why be born a chrysalis if you can never become a butterfly? Etc.

However, the chains of Love have padlocked that door now.

So, nothing: I paste on my public-relations-man smile and go out to the street.

This is the worst thing of all: to have been born in the wrong place, at the wrong . . .

▪▪▪ 60

He is tall for his age; he is slender, feline. He has green eyes, long eyelashes, darting eyebrows: he is the most beautiful child in the world. He is my son. Astute and courageous.

He generally chooses his words well. But he often prefers silence: I don't know how he learned so quickly that language is good for people to never understand. He does not talk much. He tires of talking, and I suppose he thinks that it would take too many words to explain himself. So he prefers being silent. I pray to God that we have learned to interpret his silences. He is a peaceful child who explores the world around him neither boldly nor coward-like, learning to fall in love with life, trying not to bother anyone and not wanting to be bothered by others.

He has already gotten wind of my demons and he loves me even though I am not very nice: I fear he would have preferred another father, a father less involved in the world of strange ideas and jokes that sometimes make him ask me to keep quiet. "What kind of madness makes him the way he is?" he must ask himself, but he finds he loves me despite these mysteries.

But, of course, these riddles will find their answers in dialogues between us if we find time enough. They are his and mine, no one else's.

If he comes in tonight to whisper a few words, it is because, when he was very little, he opened the front door, looked out to the mountains in the blue dusk that day, and asked me:

"Daddy . . . where was the sea the Chileans took from us? Right here, out there, or far, far away?"

SIX

It is not difficult to tolerate: my day starts at nine-thirty when I wake up, and since I have been independent for years, I can go to work whenever I want to. I get dressed, shave with an electric razor I bought in Minneapolis, and if I feel like it, I drink two or three cups of coffee with four or five cigarettes. So what? I go to work and do the same thing that, in the final analysis, everyone does: I collect, if I can and pay, if I can.

That's all, ten good hours. I eat lunch in the office because I have grown accustomed to eating alone, and then I do more of the same until six or seven o'clock. And I am almost always surprised: Is it nine o'clock already? I say out loud to myself.

I have good days and bad days. I know I am not a businessman—what is today called an executive—by nature. I am not cut out for it. But I have done it. If you visited me here you would believe it. I started out with an empty briefcase and in three years have acquired everything I need: a darkroom, an electric typewriter, an extra desk, extra furniture, extra chairs, two telephones, books, books, books. I have truckloads of bills, mine and others'. I dictate letters, correct letters, and sign letters. I take photographs, burn photographs, copy photographs, enlarge photographs . . . I collect bills, pay bills. It is all easy and all the same, day in, day out.

I have a secretary, an accountant, a draftsman, a bill collector, and a messenger. Seated at my desk, I see a crazy succession of people come and go, each with his own story. If I go out to sell, because I have finally learned to sell, I sell: selling is my business and I have learned it well.

At seven or eight or nine o'clock, I leave, cross the street and get into the car, and my family kisses me on the cheeks and fusses over me and loves me and asks me how I am and I ask, how are all of you? And we ride home in the car and if you peeked in the window you would envy me: this isn't true, this can't be true, you would say, this family is straight out of a movie. And it is straight out of a movie: if you got to know my family, you would envy me.

We get home and have dinner and then the children play house or jungle games or we watch television and crack jokes and laugh and then it is midnight and we all go peacefully to bed, the dog included, and tomorrow is another day and oh man, you never thought you would have it so good.

▪▪▪ 62

But before you lie down to sleep and before you close your eyes and before you lie there, looking at the moonlight on the ceiling, you criticize yourself: I didn't have time to write today either, you say. The blank pages are there, tucked away and clean. You get up and say: Come on, man, it's not too late; give it a try.

Then: "Daddy, don't make noise. I can't sleep."

And: "Come to bed . . . what are you doing?"

Finally: "Daddy, that's enough . . . it's so late . . ."

All right, all right, you say, I'm coming. And you go and lie down and look at the ceiling. You keep hearing it, damn it, you keep hearing it. And you will never tell a soul that that's why you get up so late in the morning.

Because you never, never did find time to sit down at the typewriter. And because, although no one will believe you, that is how everything turns to ash.

Because, damn it all, no cork can stop it.

And you can be happy for one day, your last.

Though there are times like these, when there is no "Daddy, it's so late" and no "Come to bed now."

Sometimes it happens during the day, too: there is no "Pay this bill" or no "How should we do this one?" There are days when you feel like you are dead because no one comes to bother you.

And then, yes: two or three pages get done. Mediocre ones, of course, because you have to be half-wizard, half-madman in this business, but the pages get done.

Most of all, to soothe your conscience.

But they are mediocre. Because, being a job for a porter with a magician's touch, it cannot be picked up and put down as if it were a checking account. Or a repair job on a floor polisher. Or the operation of a locomotive.

▪▪▪ 63

But day dawns and things look different: Why bother? What difference does it make? How many others have attempted the same?

And what good is it?

Aren't these three budding lives more important than your own, which you know has been going downhill for a while now? Why can't you just give up? Why not quit? By writing a paragraph today and another one a week later, you will never do any serious work, nothing that really counts or deserves to endure . . . Why not give up? Why not, you damn idiot?

Oh, what a pest.

Day dawns and your conscience bothers you because today you were supposed to go to work. Or because today you were supposed to take the children to the country. Or because today you had to sign an important contract. Because today you had to pay off a debt. Or you slept away the morning because you worked last night to soothe your conscience, and that's how it is: today it bothers you.

Good thing, that.

▪▪▪ 64

The armor has cracked, Quixote my friend, so you drink.

Some nights you flee, run away, escape.

You can't go on. You can't spread yourself thin between the song and the three budding lives that ask for things, need affection, smiles, appreciation, attention, and above all, time, the time you are so short of now, time you had to spare then, sitting around the Plaza San Martin with your bundle under your legs.

You drink. You escape some nights to talk to newspaper vendors who sleep on the sidewalks waiting for the morning edition. And to lost drunkards who sit on benches and bet about whether they will freeze that night. To displaced politicians who cry their eyes out as they recall their glory days. To those who drink in silence because they like to drink, period. Hangers-on who stay after closing time. The ones who fall asleep on the table. The taxi driver who says: "I used to read you, before you stopped publishing . . . Let's have a drink at the Plaza del Estadio." To those who live alone after divorce. The addicted. The frightful women. The misplaced persons.

You make excuses: I need to talk to my people. I need to know how the truck driver bound for Yungas feels, how the starving prostitute feels, what the alcoholic talks about as he loads crates for quick cash, what the street hawker is whispering, what curses are being ferried by the phantoms of the night.

And, of course: they blame you. That is fair. They do not hear the song.

They cannot understand you: a family straight out of a movie, and you drink. A relatively young, quasi-respected man, and you drink. You are a caricature of yourself, they tell you.

You get defensive: actually, we are all caricatures.

They argue: Why do you drink? It's a matter of will-power . . .

You swear: I'll never drink again.

You touch your ear because the words echo and you hear it again.

It is there, way back there.

And you betrayed it.

That is how it is.

That is why this is the way it is.

Right here and now, my son appears.

My typing woke him up, and his eyes are only half open.

But he comes over to my corner and says:

"Daddy, are you done yet?"

In a minute.

Time to look at the ceiling.

Because tonight there is no moonlight.

And because you still hear it, you still hear it.

What a carrot.

I think of Almaraz. Of Salazar Bondy.

Ulcers at forty. Cancer at forty. Dead at forty. And it was not suicide. What was it?

▪▪▪ 65

At the end of the third day the first sentence was served.

A sad drizzle made warm water drip from the roof tiles.

I was walking down the dark street when I saw my things bounce on the sidewalk and, in disbelief, watched as a ridiculous collection of rags and paper landed in the street in a circle of light cast from the doorway onto an old tree. People passed, stopped, listened to the old landlady curse my bad habits. "Poor woman," I remember thinking, "after all, she's right."

The things stopped piling up on the sidewalk. A little group of wide-eyed onlookers formed and I, slow of movement, sat down like a brooding hen on top of my rags and books.

Fouille's *History of Philosophy,* purchased in 1955, when I was a student. Sebastián's *Lima the Horrible,* purchased after he died, although I didn't know he had died, and my bundle of scrap paper, legal size, a leather jacket I'd brought from Bolivia, a . . . etc., etc.

I put on my jacket, picked up the books, tried stuffing some handkerchiefs into my pocket, took a shirt. I tied it all together, and seeing that nothing else would fit, I started to walk away. The onlookers continued to wait, but before I reached the corner they were divvying up the remaining junk. There wasn't much.

At night in Campo de Marte, people sleep under the trees. As if under some strange spell, every night and on every corner, the sidewalks near the Ministry of Education teem with trash and garbage, strange packages, dogs, bums, and cats, and become the resting place for everyone who has stopped choosing. There are three lengthy avenues that connect Plaza San Martin to El Callao and by night they are dark and dead; by day, dirty and hot. The parks near San Isidro, smelling of cemeteries, are big and dead by night; empty, sad, and expansive by day.

In three days and nights you can crisscross the entire city of Lima. My bundle bothered me because my fingers let go, beyond my control, but I refused to leave it in a corner: piles of garbage are mushrooms that sprout insultingly in exotic places and I did not want to consign my papers to such a fate.

I reprehended Sebastián for his recent death, the friend with many good answers to so many of my questions, the man who had held my pages in his hand one day but had died before he could keep his promise to discuss them. I thought about La Paz, asked myself what my obscure reasons for not being there were. I sniffed about Lima, a mute battlefield intersected by damp alleyways; in memory I weighed every street and avenue, every shadow.

I tried to make some sense of my two sleepless years when doctors had carried out an interminable series of experiments on me until I resigned myself to sleeping by day and living by night; finally, I fatalistically reviewed every step that had brought me to this somnambulist roaming—to such a sad and absurd end—and with these thoughts in mind, I reached the same streets where my adult life had begun, the old colonial side streets near San Martin, rife with fleabag hotels for old prostitutes and penniless bums, streets that gentlemen cross every day and timid souls avoid every night; and, sitting down on the dirty grass in the square, as though hypnotized, I looked but did not see the blinking lights and beautiful women and men's *guayaberas* and the eyes of the crazy people who cross the square each midnight; looking without thinking or feeling, defeated and overpowered, making myself believe that I truly was defeated and dreams had been nothing but dreams.

But not even then could I believe it. I could not accept it even when I sat there, not knowing where to look. It would never be as it was the first time around, when by pure chance I happened into the bookstore where my conquest of Lima had begun when they sent me, an unknown who knew no one, to *La Prensa;* because this time I knew everybody, and everybody knew me there, in that newsroom, in every paper's newsroom, and in the streets where I had learned to greet people by saying *Qué hay, patín?* and where once someone had told me that he collected all my articles.

Now I was branded, I was a Communist. I could not ask for a typewriter again or even pick up odd jobs. I would be turned away. People would recognize me, be surprised to see me resuscitated, be wary of walking beside me.

Lying on the grass, I looked at La Colmena. The world was empty and there was no place in it for me. I was afflicted, infected with political leprosy, and familiar faces passed by without looking at me, for no one looks for friends on the ground or in the shadows. Excommunication turned my face to smoke; a rubric had smashed the memory of those whose paths had crossed mine during the previous one thousand days.

So I sat for a few hours in the warm drizzle of the night and the dawn, looking at the weak lights of the Bolívar Hotel, my rags under my legs.

I had nothing to hope for and no desire to see the sun come up.

▪▪▪ 66

I am seated now in a comfortable chair, ten years older, equally foolish and hopeful, still believing in my Rocinante, the typewriter keys.

This is the third typewriter I have run into the ground. My father's typewriter doesn't count, though Tristán once told me that on it I wrote the best thing I ever did. And God knows where the best thing I ever wrote is. I left it with the rest of my things, the day I left my parents' house, and life made things and papers to disappear.

My first typewriter, which I bought in Lima, lasted four years and expired of old age in a dingy hotel in Philadelphia, writing foolish articles for a Lima newspaper. My second, which I bought in Panama, also lasted four years.

A thieving repairman lied and ruined it on the pretext that he could fix it. And the one I have now skips, because my children use it to peck out the alphabet for their half-page-long stories.

If I took five steps to the mirror now, I would see the same expression I must have had that night in Lima. Because that was the end of a road, though I thought there was a way out, and there was.

On the other hand, I already glimpse down this alley the wall that blocks the sun completely.

Two cells and three children.

In the end, fingers lose their agility and typewriter keys raise dead echoes in the night. In the end, I look down the deserted street and glance at the corner and try to imagine approaching footsteps, and I know I hear nothing, that my imagination is flagging, that the world is made differently than I had supposed, that I was mistaken, that none of what I hoped for was to be, and possibly, neither was I.

▪▪▪ 67

Let's nivolize.

Jim.

Naturally, I could never see eye to eye with Jim, nor could the man who pulls the cart ever see eye to eye with the one who rides in it, or the man who makes the cake with the one who eats it.

Although, of course, sometimes you can talk things over.

Jim has a bar near the Pan Am building in New York.

Years back, when I passed through New York every six months or so, I used to visit Jim because we had become friends five years before, when I lived on 36th Street, in a ratty hotel, writing about American newspapers.

"Hey!" Jim used to say effusively. "Hey!"

"Hi!" I would say just as effusively. "Hi!"

And he would come over, toothpaste commercial teeth, soccer player shoulders, jujitsu fighter hands, a prize athlete's waistline, dead legs hanging from a wheelchair that made a slight purring noise as it moved.

"The usual?" he would ask, although six months is six months.

"The usual," I would smile.

He would serve me a bourbon and ginger ale, and go down to the other end of the bar. Jim was a super nice guy. It was very pleasant being his friend: hey, hey and hi, hi.

One of those times, when it was snowing outside and I was half-frozen by the time I got there, I found that the snow had scared away most of the regulars, which was unusual, and we finally got to talking.

He got it wrong three times when he tried to guess where I was from. Twice, when he tried to place it on the map. I don't know how it is for you, but I think that every city in the world boils down to a couple of doors, the door to your house and the door to your job; a few faces, the faces of friends we will never forget; and the few street corners we cross every day, corners that would miss us if we went a different way. Say what you will, that's what it comes down to, whether you live in Viacha or Tokyo. At any rate, we had things in common: Jim's furniture cost him a few months' savings, and to pay the rent on his two rooms, he had to work a solid four hours a day; that was all we had.

Jim did not know much of the world: he was born in Brooklyn and he lost his legs in Saigon. He didn't even know San Francisco because the plane flew over it without stopping. He did not remember much about Saigon because he got there at the end of the grand finale.

"Twelve days later," he slapped his palms, "it was all over and we left."

He caught me looking at my bourbon. That got him started.

"Don't think I regret it," he said angrily. "Don't think for a moment that I lost my legs for nothing. I was a champ in Brooklyn and would have gone into the professional leagues. But don't you think I lost them for nothing, fella. I thought so once, on the stretcher and in the hospital, because they also took out a big piece of my gut . . . I thought so until I came home and saw my children in the park. And I realized that they still had that look in their eyes because I had lost my legs way over on the other side of the world. I realized that, somehow, my legs paid for that look in their eyes. My legs, my buddies' arms, and my friends' eyes, the crosses we left all over the place . . . my legs paid for their look, you know? And because of my dead legs, millions of children have a right to that look. Because, if I hadn't lost them, maybe the children would have lost it all. We stopped those damn guys over there, and that's where they stayed. Of course, they want to come over here, but they'll never come, you know. They'll never come here, because the kids know I gave my legs for that look in their eyes, you know, and they would give me their lives, if they had to, to keep that look alive . . . a little tough, because it's difficult to be boss of the world . . . but there's nothing worse than a loser, and my legs made sure those kids weren't losers . . ."

He smiled, his eyes bright. "Want another?"

I nodded. Cross-cultural communication is no easy matter; you have to work at it. I was frightened by his hands, huge, near, and heavy. He understood my initial reaction. We both tried and then we spent many hours discussing this Saigon business from a thousand different angles and arguing like maniacs because, as I said, we could never be on the same side of the trenches. But we could talk: that much we could do.

It's odd: I have remembered Jim for a very long time.

▪▪▪ 68

But Jim was mistaken; there is a look that is better than the one in the eyes of his children, the bosses of the world. There is a look as transparent as the one in his children's eyes, only cleaner, purer, stronger.

It is the look in my son's eyes, my son who asked about the sea, who cried in a corner, and who walks around now, stealthy as a cat, not bothering anyone and not allowing anyone to bother him.

It is better because he already knows the Beast and keeps on living, perhaps not being as afraid of the Beast as I am.

And it is better because he does not let the big, old lies bother him. Maybe, if he feels very lonely one day, they will, but I doubt it.

His look is better because it is innocent. It is better than the look in the eyes of the bosses of the world because he is not to blame, nor does he inherit blame. His look still holds a harmony that perhaps no man can touch or destroy.

He is not an accomplice.

▪▪▪ 69

My son's enemy is still there, in a plain bureaucrat's office, looking at his hands, which other executioners have mangled.

His eyes leave his claws and stare at the wall. In the slits above his pronounced cheekbones, two sparks of rage appear. Perhaps he remembers his former cell and still feels

the unbearable pain that rained on him when he was behind bars in the cage from which he emerged, bones and
spirit broken. The pain killed everything; all that remains
now is his need to grab hold of objects like an old bear
and his vision of an endless war in which there are only
victims and executioners.

In his world, one can only survive by being an
executioner.

This wild barbarian, this faceless warrior is the heir
apparent to twenty centuries of our common memory.
Disguised in civilian dress, he perpetuates the attitudes
he learned while abusing his uniform, another of his dis-
guises that dehumanize and deny his individuality in order to ensure the mass complicity of the professionals of
crime. He looks as cold as an eel and imitates the indifference of a machine; trained by professionals arrived from
distant shores, he implements an art and science whose
perfection is the clearest sign of our times.

When he stands up, he shakes with rage and shouts
hysterically:

"One more word, just one more word and . . ."

Yet, even this screeching sounds like acquired learning; he knows perfectly well that I am in his hands, that I
am his prey in this dark cell, or in the Big Cell outside.

It is all but impossible to believe that he will be forever
victorious simply because he can kill, and because therein
lies his superiority, and because his enemies will never be
capable of killing, believing that therein lies their own
superiority.

▪▪▪ 70

The Weaknesses of Fiction:

The daily heroism displayed by man's son is simple,
straightforward, and even boring on occasion, isn't it?

It does not transcend the anecdotal, although it sustains the Universe, our Universe.

You say to yourself: " . . . but if this man is merely like me, how can he save the world?"

"I like the other kind of heroism, the Heroism found in thick books," somebody states.

But let's forget for a moment about the Patriarch, the Buccaneer who creates Companies, the Founder of Empires, the Comrade-at-Arms, the Intrepid General, the Mother-Soldier.

Today, and on a whim, let us salute man's son.

Yes, the man who walks hunched over down the street, who has children, educates them, pays what he owes, and believes that tomorrow everything will be different.

Merely because he sustains the Universe.

"I salute you, unknown hero."

There: now we feel better.

SEVEN

Yet, all things considered, I can say without hesitation that there are moments when, despite everything, I am happy. And what's more, that I am happy because I am prisoner to my three children. That with each passing day of their becoming they make me happy and have made me happy every day since they came one by one into the world, inexpressible surprise.

This happiness is, as you know, made of shared moments.

Of sentences:

"Who discovered America?"

She, fearing she had committed the Great Wrong: "It wasn't me!"

She was three years old.

"I'm not going to school anymore; the teacher asks about everything and I don't know nothing."

She was five. And at the age of four:

"Let me tell you my *soñanzas,* my dreamhopes . . .

One forgets these things, but we live off them. And continue living because of them.

Thus, seeing my days in this light, there are no mad chains shackling me to these four walls.

Only when I start thinking.

Only when I start imagining the three of them, grown. And only when I think of the days to come.

But, for now, it is beautiful: I spend my nights telling the adventures of The Little Red Indian Girl and The Big, Bad Balloon. And I listen and see how, without realizing it or knowing it, they devour their days, become part of this, their world, get to know it and take hold of it, as I did in my day.

Eventually, a day will come when, without knowing it or realizing it, they will say: I am from here. They will find, as I did in my time, that they made the wrong choice, that they closed the doors of Day, that they chose for themselves and their children and their children's children the lot of the oppressed, the condition of the exploited, the thin loaf of the perennially robbed, the sadness of those who live a life that is not right, that will never be right, and that nothing could ever change their lot.

Strangest of all, they will learn to love their lot.

It will be as it was with me in Barcelona, when, contemplating going North to explore it and find my place in the sun, I decided—I don't understand why—to turn back to the Night. And to be yet another citizen of Night. To share with them this perpetual sadness of mine, of knowing that I am a citizen of Night.

And to learn to give up this rebelliousness preached everywhere in lieu of telling another story about The Little Red Indian Girl and The Big, Bad Balloon. Stories that are happy, as the names suggest. And lives that are happy and joyful, just as they appear to be, until the time comes when the discovery of Night's citizenship lends a patina of sadness to our eyes.

To everyone's eyes. All you have to do to see it is walk out in the street.

After recognizing oneself in those eyes, how could anyone take public office?

Passing by, my friends wink at me and consider me a failure.

And you know, maybe I am.

Who would ever have imagined that you can weave failure with short stories about The Little Red Indian Girl and The Big, Bad Balloon?

▪▪▪ 72

. . . when it came to them, my friend, we decided on the French for their miseducation.

And the clever French are here, playing the conquerors in this satrapy and disseminating their culture in the unseeded soil of children's souls. At the proper time, skin color will make the difference.

They will find, as I did, that there is nowhere they belong, that they are foreigners here because they were given a Gallic soul, yet they don't belong there because they were not born there. Which is what happened with me, only they will speak French in the end.

Yet, what is the alternative?

With the French, there still is the hope that they can conquer Day's citizenship and come back later as visitors of Night, I console myself.

Though I know that is not how it happens. When I visit them in other places, my Brothers and Sisters ask for an old newspaper, an outdated magazine, or a picture of the Mountain . . . Here, the Brothers and Sisters of my Greater Family do nothing but loiter about and steal from one another and never, ever change things; elsewhere, wherever that may be, they bemoan their lost, exploited, and impoverished country, or they bastardize themselves: they put on foreign accents and disguise themselves in every way, except for skin color . . . they are the legion of the lost.

This sadness of finding ourselves forced to work to commit suicide as individuals and as a people, of negating ourselves as one and as all, seems to be part of the price we must pay to put a piece of bread in our mouth.

We are all the same in this; the only thing that varies is the intensity of this negation and the quality of the bread.

We have never been able to reject this denial.

Nor have we been able to earn our bread by other means.

Thus I, who picked the prison I have chosen, try to teach them something different: Your native land is the place where you can feel comfortable, I tell them, the place where you feel you belong, you know you can grow. Like my father, I know that I shall fail in this attempt.

Native land to them, to myself, and to my father has been a constant, keen sore place in the heart. A great sorrow. A pit of horrible misfortune.

My tragedy is to have inherited this sorrow as it always was.

My shame will be to leave this same soreness to my children.

My treachery is to know it and not do what I must to change everything.

I chose a futureless present of happy and joyful days instead of a future emerging from a present made up of tragedy, sacrifice, and heroism.

This option explains a racist, unjust, suicidal, and self-destructive society: it is not only my personal choice, it is part of our national character.

What is the alternative? I was asking.

I know because I have already seen that some people will deride me and charge that my question implies, in some way, a denial of all alternatives.

They will speak to me of ideologies. They will sing

me brave songs of unknown heroes. They will tell me that one must read thick books in order to identify the alternatives.

To which I, twenty years older now, say: Show me, my friend, the thick book read by the "Republiquetas," those Freedom Riders who paved the way for our political independence. Show me, my friend, the thick book read by the Vietnamese Montagnards. Show me, friend, the thick book read by the Cubans of Sierra Maestra.

Don't lie to me anymore, friends.

They needed no thick books.

Not at all.

As his murder in our midst—we all know who—was not pure chance, either.

Him.

It was, Brothers and Sisters, our complicity.

This complicity that keeps coming with us from the day we were born and that will keep going with us until the day we die.

As one.

And as all.

■■■ 73

The above, Mr. Chief of National Security, is not a confession that I have been, am now, or ever will be a Communist.

I insist: I have not been, am not now, and will not be a Communist.

Because that is not my problem.

My problem is how to feed my people.

How in the hell to feed them.

Feed. Them.

That is it, in a word.

And brother, just guess what you can do with the words you say and speak and shout in semi-deserted town squares; with your repulsive ways of getting a loaf of bread, a beer, a gun.

Ideologies.

Brother, you see, I have already said that there is hate to spare in our love of one another.

This brotherly and plentiful hate that is in short supply only where supplies are an anomaly: among those of our backward brothers and sisters who have not learned even to recount their tragedy.

Among them, who are the source of our guilt, there is no hate, no hope, no tomorrow.

Think of them later, when you put your bread in your mouth.

No.

To live without the song is not easy at all.

It has a price, Brother.

▪▪▪ 74

As I was saying:

Constant fear was wearing me down. Most of all, because the Beast could kill me before it ever had a chance to read. Locked up, in the first cell, I looked across the yard at the Beast and reconstructed my crime: "The real cause of this crisis is corruption in the highest levels of government." I already said that.

I also said that thanks to my luck and my friends, my time in jail is hardly worth remembering; in a country where naked people are hurled alive from planes into the Sacred Lake or an impenetrable jungle, we cannot exactly say that these cells were a Via Dolorosa, can we?

But the true fear was the fear of dying identified with the Beast.

After all, reading may have not given me the keys to posterity, if there still is such a thing, but violence was never a valid argument in my debating ways, not even when violence was perpetrated against me, nor when I was forced to go hungry, nor when I was cheated and robbed, nor when I realized I was a naked citizen of Night.

But there and then I was at the mercy of the Beast.

What strange pride made me scorn the fear of death and an animal's death among animals?

But how should we react when we are captives of the Beast?

"They will not get near me," I swore. The Beast will not get near me.

I smoked like a chimney and, taking big steps, paced from wall to wall, where I was not prepared to react as one should fearing the abrupt entry of the Beast there, and he would kick journalism into me, beating me until he squashed me like a frog.

Naturally, the last people on earth who could have taught me how to react at times like these were my friends and colleagues: they wrestled, as I did, with words.

So if it was a question of bursting, I decided, the best thing to do would be to burst my own way.

I cracked my sunglasses and tried to slit my wrists.

▪▪▪ 75

The scene: a room measuring seven by five meters. A thin wood floor that had seen better days, but long ago; windows facing the street, blocked with bricks; windows facing the yard, boarded up with planks. In one corner, a broken wooden cot; a broken high-backed chair held together with wire. Walls covered in pink wallpaper on which nails, fingers, and combs had scratched drawings and strange messages; dried bloodstains and traces of shit and urine on the floor, walls, and ceiling. The permanent, unmistakable print of a bare foot in a streak of sunlight. Marks in the old planks left by the legs of an electric stove.

An extinguished light bulb hanging from a spiderweb of wire. A smell of cold, of white lilies, of the obscene breath of pain and suffering. Mute echoes of shrieking in the corners. This is the kingdom of the Beast, Brothers and Sisters; this is where your tax money goes.

Slitting your wrists is difficult. You must press resolutely and firmly. But it is not impossible; it's a question of persistence. The blood spurts, blotting in red the old black stains. The blood is warm on your arm, under your white shirtsleeve, on your elegant slacks, on your knee. A ray of sun reflected on the floor, dust particles dance in the yellow beam that disappears in the blinking of an eye, for the night pervades all. Gradually, darkness.

But, I swore, the Beast will not get near me.

▪▪▪ 76

She is sleeping.

Ten years earlier, in a narrow and dark room, he heard a woman's voice:

"Telephone!"

And then her voice, far away:

"You said you were coming, but you didn't."

How could I go back? I couldn't go back. I was unable to work for eleven months. The sad months, when white hairs sprouted in my red beard. I spent my days stretched out on a rickety old bed and my nights walking like a wolf through deserted streets. I could not go back.

"And since you didn't come back like you promised you would, I'm coming there. I'm arriving the twenty-third, at four in the afternoon."

It's madness, I thought. They won't let her. To come all the way here, to find me in the state she knows I'm in . . . No. She won't come. I returned to my cave. To my cot. She won't come, I thought many times; it would be madness.

But she came. And she helped me step out of the trap.

She washed me, cleaned me, talked to me as one talks to a child, saved me.

I ventured out to find work. Once again.

She is still here, ten years later, asking, when it gets late:

"When are you going to sleep? Come to bed. Stop writing now. You can get back to it tomorrow."

We started out utterly naked, poor. We kept on, just as poor, less naked. She bore our children. She is here, with me. I cannot sleep, because I am still banging away at the typewriter.

But, thank God, she is here.

That's something.

▪▪▪ 77

Then the troubles that followed, and even those that had preceded, opened a chink in the armor: you drink.

That is why now, at this very moment, she comes in and takes the bottle away.

She does not understand my bad habit.

She does not understand the chink in the armor.

But she is right.

The only advantage she has is that she can sleep.

Perhaps her song is different.

It could be.

▪▪▪ 78

"Qué hay, patín?"

José Claudio, an elephant in a yellow raincoat, in the drizzling rain. Hands in his pockets. Ice blue eyes, thick glasses.

Surprised, I looked at him. He was the last person I expected to see. He smiled a half-cynical smile, almost shyly.

Here we go, I said.

"Doesn't look like you're headed anywhere."

No.

"I'm going home."

That's nice. I'm not.

"Can I treat you to coffee?"

I had worked for him three times in the past, so I knew him. But he seemed polite. Maybe he was lonely that night.

All right . . . Thanks.

I stood up and, still uncertain, lagged behind him as we crossed San Martin. For the few blocks until we got to the Chinese restaurant, I remembered him while looking at his huge back.

Christmas, two years before, he and I together, all night long. In the morgue, looking at corpses and listening to his sick jokes. I was living alone in Lima. He wasn't. The teletype, his fit of rage, my dismissal and immediate reinstatement, a bottle of warm beer . . . His damn habit of making us stay at the office all night because he liked to take us out for breakfast at the hotel around the corner. He was young, arbitrary, important. Unpleasant, rude, and talented. His life and mine had crossed paths every so often. And here he was now, out for a dawn walk, a huge butterball with a few strands of tow-colored hair, his hands in the pockets of a wrinkled, expensive blue suit, a fancy tie— stained, perhaps—with his pampered child's cheeks and his faraway eyes, blue slits behind Japanese commando glasses.

He ordered something, a cup of coffee. He leaned his elbows on the table and looked at me, curious. He noticed my bundle, on the chair, and surmised the rest. I lit a butt. I looked at him; he waited: the price of my coffee was my story.

A short story. I hurled it at him in a diatribe of righteous, useless indignation. I protested against my sentence. I protested against Peru's sentence, its long suffering. Against Lima's nightlife of lunatics, bums, prostitutes, degenerates. Against my long road, against the random event that sent me packing; against the hard, absurd road marked by injustices that I had to walk just for being born where I was born.

I talked about my two good years: the embassy and the newspaper. Barking with laughter, I related the story of Belaunde's gonads. I noted that friends had deserted me. I underlined the ways I had tried to overcome my sentence, sidestep the blacklist and find a job, any job. I cataloged the slow and awkward loss of the things that make life more pleasant, things that were expensive in the beginning and worthless to the pawnbroker. I said I was convinced that, when one comes up against them—"What do you mean, 'them'?" he asked, uncertain—you cannot win, no matter what you do.

I summarized my days and nights in the windowless room, trading translations for money and money for black tobacco cigarettes, Sublime-brand chocolates, and slices of meat from the stand on the corner. I repeated some sad monologues from my night walks by the dirty sea, I fleetingly mentioned the sonorous voices of obsessive memories, and I said to him, accepting my lot without further motivation to continue struggling: ". . . and this is how it all ends," my cigarette butt pointing at the bundle of scrap paper.

He did not say a word for a long while. Then he decided, on impulse. He spread out some little white magic bags on the table. And, about this mountain of plastic envelopes, he said:

"What are you so bitter about? This is the best answer!"

Furious, I pontificated. I upbraided him for his mansion

in Miraflores. His millions, his seal, and his coat of arms. I accused him of being heir and beneficiary of a system that worked for him and crushed me, of wasting his talent, education, and intelligence. Oh, if only I were him, muttered a voice in a dark corner of my brain; if only I had a year, just one of the years he squanders! I inveighed him to do his duty to this, his world of drizzling rain and poverty, of lunacy and horrible cruelty, and to himself, a writer and journalist who was still young—he was scarcely past twenty—and I bravely insulted him for his addiction, and then fell silent, staring with a sickening feeling at the little envelopes which, I knew, had sown terror and mourning, suicide and tears among my professional colleagues.

He said nothing when it was over. He listened to me politely, patiently let me finish. He put the envelopes back in his pocket, hung his tow-haired head, and stood up.

"Call me tomorrow."

He started to leave when, as if suddenly remembering something, he turned around to leave me some bills on the table.

"It's only a loan, naturally."

Alone, I ordered a pack of good cigarettes, stretched out my legs, and ordered a second cup of coffee. My mind was blank.

Darkness was in its final throes when I went outside and the bellowing of city routines had begun. Weariness overcame me. I checked into the Oriental Hotel in Chinatown. It had been my sanctuary a few times before and I felt comfortable there. I slept all day because José Claudio's day begins when everyone else's day ends. That was the last job José Claudio gave me.

At dusk, when I washed my face, I heard it again. It was right there.

In my bundle of dirty clothes and scrap paper.

▪▪▪ 79

A year later, well-fed and not overly soused, we were sitting in our underwear in a cabin north of New York. We
were looking at the fire, the snowflakes, the huge moon.

It was Harry's cabin, but we had not known until he
showed up there that he was joining us for dinner. I had
been traveling at José Claudio's expense, at Harry's expense, and was trying to digest fourteen months of places,
interviews, solitude, drunken sprees, women, study, and
other things we had seen on our tour of Day. José Claudio
came, on vacation; Harry was sleeping, and now the evening was over, the wining and dining and long, near-joyful
conversation ended.

He looked at me again from behind his thick glasses, a
calm look, cold blue slits, baby cheeks.

"There is nothing for us here . . . nothing for me," I
said, trying to coax an opinion out of him.

As before, he looked at me and said nothing.

"They showed us the Big Pie, but we are only visitors
from the Night. Night citizens, fortunate enough to have
been invited to visit Day. Which is the last word? That
I am a demi-man visiting the world of demi-gods? Have
they shown me Day only to teach me that I will never
be able to face them, that I should go back to my Night?
What should I do?"

"It's a problem for each person's conscience," he said
in a low voice.

He finished his drink a while later. "Good night." He
stood up, a fat, unclothed giant made of butter. He turned
around and I saw his scar, a purple snaking line starting
near his neck and ending between his buttocks.

"José Claudio . . ."

Without turning around, he told me about it:

"An accident. Pain. That is how this business of the

little white bags got started, the business that brought you here."

And he went to bed.

He left the next day without saying good-bye because he thought I was asleep. I did not see him again. Just his voice when I phoned him from the airport, years later.

"How dare you call me so early?" he said, and hung up. It was three o'clock in the afternoon.

I went back to my plane and returned to my mountains, annoyed because, after having given me so much, he had refused to give me his friendship.

I don't think it was anything personal. He was very busy living his life and I had nothing to offer him.

I am going through the same thing now. I understand him, finally. I understand why José Claudio was never my friend. Why Salazar died before he found the time to discuss my bundle of scrap paper.

Nothing personal.

It is, quite simply, that there are things you learn in solitude, in silence, in egotism, in the irate defense you put up against the world. Things that no one can teach. Like the bad habit of writing.

Or like the song.

■ ■ ■ 80

I saw him by chance eight years later. On Comercio Street.

That is, I saw his book.

In a pretty window. In the center. As if he were looking at me, face to face, and I felt like he was scolding me.

Because his book tells me that he always knew what he had to do. He always knew he was a citizen of Night. He, who was born privileged and possessed a huge fortune.

He, the system's beneficiary and heir, had always known he was a struggling citizen of Night.

Here he is now, thick glasses and baby cheeks, blue ice swirls in his eyes, displaying the mask he wears as a face, above a list of his book titles.

At last I know what he already knew in New York. The reason he never wanted to be my friend.

He was never prisoner to two cells and three children.

He must have a different way of loving.

He must have found the road to freedom.

I never found mine.

EIGHT

■■■ 81

He was born in 1912. He was never very certain of where he belonged. Perhaps he died before he could discover that he did not belong anywhere. Or perhaps he was right when he told us that he belonged to this place. He was, however, a strange breed: he was a member of the middle class when no middle class existed. And he was a perfect gentleman, save for one essential detail: he was always broke. He was an educated man, but his education included the knowledge that where he lived, his education was totally or practically useless.

He was white, which was supposed to be an advantage then. He was a mestizo, a fact betrayed only by his love for *aji* and *jallpahuaica*. The mixture had happened way back, back in Salta. But there it was, it was there.

He taught me: "Don't ever get mixed up in politics, because it's no place for decent men." By the sixth time he repeated it, I replied, and by then I knew how to read: "But if you leave politics to indecent men, you hand them the country on a platter." He did not know what to answer.

His heroism had nothing to do with bullets. It had to do with bread: the bread he put on the table for forty years until, a defeated and broken man, his heart burst in anguish.

He was good: he believed in God. Later on, he thought, when things got out of man's control, they would be in God's hands. He was not like his wife, who exaggerates all extremes: "Be patient," she would say, as if her words were the philosopher's stone.

But, of course, he was mistaken.

I do not know why he went to war. I do not remember him ever telling us about civic duty. For the same reason, perhaps, that he never told us about sex: maybe he did not know how to broach the subject with children. And yet, one day while we were playing soccer in the garden, I spotted the trace of patriotism under his arm: a Paraguayan machine gun had pumped a slug there, and there it remained for his entire life. Other people told me something about it. He himself never breathed a word.

I do not do what I do on account of anything he said.

I do what I do on account of what I saw him do.

And on account of what other people tell me he did. On account of things that his wife, my mother, told me he did. For, having taken him as something of a joke while he was alive, I started to take him seriously after his death. Because there are things we learn before learning what there is to learn, and those things are never subject to change.

But I am little more than his shadow. And sometimes I think I do not even come close. We all followed in his footsteps down a road of solitude, but his solitude was deeper, because no one did for him what he did for us: he gave us a happy childhood. Or perhaps we only thought he did and perhaps we are discovering now that he did not even do that. Though I think he did. I think he did with me, anyway.

His was an immense solitude, because if you could not find people like him in my day, I can just imagine how it was in his day, when wanting a roof over your head was asking for the moon, and brown skin did not go to college; when our rich uncles sent us fruit, carried overland by an Indian who would sleep on the doorstep with the dogs, the whole pack covered by snow on some mornings. Life for us has been smoother.

I do not know whether he did the right thing. Perhaps he only tried to do what he thought he should have done. I know that he thought he did not succeed in that, because I know that being certain of his failure is what killed him. And yet, as his widow says, maybe he was wrong about that. Maybe he died thinking only that he had missed the mark, and maybe it has taken us twenty years to finally clear our doubts. Today, when I see what it was, how it was, what we have become, I think that maybe he was wrong to the end; maybe he simply did what he had to do and maybe he has not disappeared without a trace. Not entirely.

Personally, I have no reason to love this place. No rational reason. I do love it, but if I stop to think it over, I ought not to love this place.

Perhaps he had an answer. And perhaps it worked for him. If things did not work out better, perhaps that is because it was not a great answer.

He did his part. But other people let him down. It's that simple. But he was convinced that he belonged in this place: after all, his friends could say the same thing; he had two. The clever one left for Brazil and the foolish one died as he did: stripped, stricken, stung, drained, and his heart overcome by grief.

He was, of course, a mining engineer. What else could he have been? His heroism is stamped in landmarks that are mere words to the rest of us: oil pipeline, tin, pyrite, cable ferry, cordillera. I went with him one day to the big mountain, but by then his heart was rent, and we had to turn back. And sometimes I saw him walking home alone at dawn, freezing and alone, returning from measuring others' property. For, the saying about the camel and needle's eye was a truth as bright as the sun in his life. So he pushed his camel through the eye of the needle, but it wasn't easy, not by any means.

His was the first death I saw. And being who he was to me, who he still is, he dies his death in me every day. It is a death that does not stop dying. It has sentenced me to relive one death forever: his death.

Every morning he is alive and every afternoon he dies, and every time I think of him he is dead but he does not die because I think of him every morning and bury him every afternoon, although he is always there again, waiting for me to awaken and think of him again. So, having died as he did, he will never die until I do.

Some days I think well of him, other days ill, sometimes I criticize him and discredit his days, sometimes I admire him, some days I do not know how things were for him, but he is with me now, here and now, with me and dead. Yet alive, because I see him laughing, for that man knew how to laugh like a child. When I was no more than a child my conscience was already mischievous and confused, and he laughed; and so with a child's eyes I see my dead father, who perhaps was mistaken, perhaps even mistaken in his love for me, but who was able to give me so much love that it still lasts.

In this way we are bound, he to me because he loved me so much and I to him because I never could love him as well.

Since I, as I say, am not even a shadow of the man.

■ ■ ■ 82

But the night passed and nothing happened: the blood dried on my shirt, the sleeves got slightly soiled, and I woke up because the cuts burned. I could not do it. Nor would I ever be able to do it, because I dreamt about him asking me where the sea was, the sea the Chileans took from us. And because my body simply refused to spurt more blood. I felt like a fool: my shirt sleeves red, my cut wounds closed, an eternal, sad, nearly noiseless rain; a big cell, dark and empty.

I took six steps. I peered out the door, to the yard down below. A woman was selling food, coffee, *api*. The guards were leaning against the walls, to get out of the rain. Their work is not tiring. A few hours of waiting, a few hours of murdering, beating, or merely frightening the cell dwellers. Sometimes they leave. And they return with one more. Or with a few more. They never identify themselves. They have a curious approach to their criminal calling: "We are under orders not to identify ourselves," they say. Sometimes they are called upon and they slip into a cell. And then you hear shouts, shrieks, moans.

At night, they rattle fat key rings, bang on chains and locks, kick the doors, open and shut the bars at whim, so as to waken those who are half-asleep in the cells. They have no alcohol. They have weapons. On occasion they shout out a name. And one man gets up, adjusts his mattress, packs his things, and steps outside. He mumbles a few words, leaves his cigarettes behind, vanishes. During the day, all you can do is pace. Pace inside the cage. Or in the yard. Or go to the corners to urinate.

When blankets are brought for us, they give them to us. But they steal cigarettes, money, cookies. Later, they sell it all back to the prisoners. They are generally strong. They are fat and tough. Only their animal expression makes you wish you had been born in another country.

For it is shameful to recognize one's own features in theirs. The cheekbones. And to eat out of tins the food that you ordinarily eat outdoors, on an umbrella-filled veranda awash in bright sunlight, drinking beer with friends. The cruel destiny that made us Kin is shameful.

Spying on them hour after hour, observing them in their daily rounds, makes you realize finally that you are in a zoo, looking at them from your cage. It takes a few hours. Maybe a few days, but that is all. It sinks in, although it is difficult to accept. I was not tortured nor was I beaten; I did not see my own blood nor did I shriek piteously. Mine was but a small lesson.

I had to learn that the world is one huge and savage cage, that nothing had changed in twenty centuries. If I learned my lesson I could go out in the street again, to live in the big cage. I knew that I was spying, not because they had forgotten about me in the black cell, but because they wanted me to spy. Because every time the Beasts passed my door, they wanted me to tremble for fear that they would rush in all at once to give me a lesson in journalism. That was the idea, and it worked. They knew, and I know, that I do not have an ideology that can strengthen my kidneys. That I am neither a rabid hater nor a fanatic. I had done and written something accurate, but writing accurately is a luxury none can afford. I had merely managed to annoy a temporary power-wielder. To become a mosquito in some important nose.

So the lesson proceeded. For the moment, just hunger and thirst. Two days of hunger and thirst is nothing. Without cigarettes, a nuisance. In the cold, walking back and forth between the walls, patting them with my hands.

I rolled down my sleeves because I did not want them to see what I had attempted to do. I was cold. I put on my jacket, my overcoat. I felt naked, inert. Empty, under the thumb of the Beast.

The lesson, then, is this: Because this is where you were born, you have no rights. And if you are lucky, you will get shot fast.

You were never born, you never lived, you were never anything, because you are here. You must learn that if you ever walk the streets again, you must show gratitude to the Beast: he was lenient. You must learn that at the end of your ten thousand days, there is nothing but this: the cage, this one or the other one, in the city or the world, and the Beast will always be on the other side of the wall. You will learn: all you have read is a tiresome tumor. You will remember: all you have seen is a meaningless goiter. You will accept: thinking is an irritating rash. Pride? All pride ends here. Better to have been born a Beast and never to have held a book in one's hands.

That is the lesson.

Leaning against the walls, moving lazily between the cages and across the yard, beneath a cold, silent, perpetual rain, they are the masters of the world. This is their world. And you will have to watch them pass, eat and laugh and smoke until you finally learn: such is their world.

Your world.

And there is no other.

▪▪▪ 83

Twelve years earlier, and with a journalist calling card, you visited Tatán on the weekends, to play chess. It was the same prison, perhaps larger and more cruel. But it was the same. Tatán was a common criminal. A bright, tidy, elegant, and famous common criminal. Thief, mugger, pickpocket, and nice guy. He was educated on the streets. He was remarkably intelligent; his fate, certain: as we played chess during those weeks, he always said the same thing:

"The only way I'll ever get out is feet first."

And he played on, chatted, smoked light tobacco cigarettes, smelled of French perfume, collected funny stories.

His career was a long one, lasting more than thirty

years. A career that bordered on legend. Escapes, bank robberies, near-perfect heists. Tunnels, spidermen, divers, famous jewels, impressive booty. His weakness: his refusal to kill, shed blood, or commit a needless act of cruelty. His brain had saved his life for decades: his attorneys followed his orders, and the law could not touch the legendary Tatán, common criminal.

They finished him off. They came to take him away one night and he clutched the bars, screaming that they were going to murder him, but they pried his fingers loose, left him unconscious, changed his cage, and locked him up among his enemies.

Some nights later the door to his new cell opened miraculously because, miraculously, his enemies circulated freely between the cells and the hallways, and at long last the law evened the score with the legendary Tatán.

He shrieked to his death from the third floor of the jailhouse. He lingered for a few hours. He looked at the world from a skeletal husk, and I remembered:

". . . feet first."

That was his world. My world. Our world.

And there is no other.

▪▪▪ 84

In Tatán's skin, but without his legend, without his experiences of daily living in one cell after another and the guards and the legal crimes, not in the habit of being Tatán, I find it nearly impossible to believe that the distance from my cell door to the yard downstairs is the same as it was for him. All I can do is remember Tatán's eyes in his crushed, amorphous face looking out at the world, and be astonished at how his brain ordered his eyes to keep blinking. And an imagination that can invent the song can also suffer Tatán's death, not once but a thousand times over. The Beast cannot have so much imagination. That is why he is a Beast. If he had any imagination, he could never, ever be the Beast.

To a man whose imagination was always the most valued haven in his life, Tatán's death appeared and reappeared, day and night, in the rain and behind the locked cell door, which his mind kept imagining had suddenly swung open.

By nightfall, the thought of dying like Tatán seemed acceptable. Only a smooth, warm, barely perceptible feeling of protest fluttered there, in a far corner of my thoughts.

This is not fair, I said. I am not Tatán. If this is how they deal with me, what hope is there for my Brothers and Sisters who rush about outside, without a clue as to where they are headed?

And why, in the end, was I hoodwinked? Why was I told that the world, our world, was different? Who invented so many ideals, so many dreams, so many false ambitions? Why didn't anyone tell me that these were the rules of the game?

Above all, why wasn't I warned in time, before I too had children? Now that my life and death are no longer in my hands, how could it be that in ten thousand days no one ever told me what our world was all about?

Two cells and three children.

By nighttime, I found nesting in the shadows the conviction that everything was a matter of chance. Let them do as they please, my mind said, there is nothing to be done. If you live, try not to feel guilty over being alive; if they kill you, try not to feel guilty over dying. I touched the cuts on my wrist and was embarrassed. I lay down on the floor, huddled in a ball, and stared at a thread of weak light stealing through the window.

A new inkling crept into my thoughts: the idea that one is never in control of oneself, that there are fears greater than one's own fear of death.

Of course, I did not know yet that they were going to sentence me to life.

I was just beginning to learn that, prisoner of others, our freedom hems us in.

How absurd the very idea of freedom is.

Helplessly imprisoned, I am shackled by the blood coursing through my veins.

How absurd it is, not being able to choose our blood. And how human, to love it anyway.

Our blood.

■ ■ ■ 85

I remember the Mississippi Delta. In their sincere desire to show us everything, my friends wanted to show me their poor people, too. For, ashamed of being so well-off, they have reserved pockets of poverty for the tourists' pleasure.

You can find out for yourself about what goes on in the Mississippi Delta and in other God-forsaken places. *Let Us Now Praise Famous Men* is the Mississippi Delta area's equivalent to *Lima the Horrible*. It is not difficult to find. Nor is it very expensive.

When you visit the Delta, you see a town of whites abandoned to their fate, mountain people with corncob pipes and lost looks, children of weakened mind and limb who cannot speak well and whose bodies are deformed: they have one arm longer than the other, some are bald, others cross-eyed, many toothless, with legs that are coiled like so many yards of twine. Their heads are always bowed because they cannot raise them. It is a place full of children and old people because neither children nor old people can get away from there.

Travelers hurry past to look at them, but to look, no more. These people are wealth's strange specimens. They never had anything in their air, water, soil, or subsoil worth stealing. And that is why there are no factories, hotels, or cities there. Nor is there any pity, of course. The world passes by in fancy cars for a short dose of cheap horror and they stare mutely when hardy gringos with perfect teeth and enviable health cruise by in their station wagons full of babies, children, and old ladies who get out from time to time to snap pictures.

When you are a guest in the land of plenty and have spent several months in Holiday Inns and Hiltons, you react almost exactly like the gringos in their station wagons: Why must you be shown these deformed children and blind, mute, awkward old people?

How pleasant it is to leave the Mississippi Delta behind after spending a day there feeling grateful that the Good Lord gave you all your limbs in the right places, that your eyes are not crusty with pus and have seen something other than a never-ending night, that you can move your legs with ease, even dance and swim in the pools of the Caribbean.

This visit is yet another way the richest country in the world sells itself to visitors. Misery has not disappeared, which only goes to show that the conquest of plenty was not easy, not at all. Admirable, isn't it?

The bad part, once again, is your imagination: And what if I was one of those children? Oh, how lucky I am, not to be! And now: on to Miami! The foolish part, once again, is the memory of it. What good does remembering do? The terrible part, too, is the certainty that to the very young and the very old of the Mississippi Delta, these words have a meaning that we visitors will never understand: It will be this way forever.

It is a forever without hope, I say, because the rich will never come to steal the riches that may be found here: there aren't any riches, none have been discovered for two hundred years. Therefore, there will never be progress. No one will come to treat the eyes covered with pus. The eyes whose only function is to sell horror to tourists, at a dollar a snapshot.

It is a forever that is different from ours; it is absolute.

It is the measure of man, a wolf to man.

▪▪▪ 86

I remember the countryside north of Santa Cruz. We flew above the green savannas in a jet that belonged to my boss's friend: in the air, music, Panama hats, laughter, and whiskey. It was like another country. He was from Santa Cruz and took great pride in pointing to all the progress. There is wealth to steal there, so wealth had come to foment progress.

It was an exciting day. I was happy.

But, at the end of the day, and as we were eating, beneath the palm trees, in our shirt sleeves and looking at beautiful women, a boy came out from the shadows and ruined it all. Silently he stepped forward, knelt down at my feet, and shined my shoes. I looked at his chest, observed his shaven head, the aged look in his eyes like the look in the eyes of poor children the world over, and I foresaw the life ahead of him.

In four sentences I deflated my boss's optimism, because what we had seen in a day of flying was never to be for that child. It was for my friends, up there, in Day. The boy was a citizen of Night, like me.

We walked later through the same places and became concerned: progress was manufacturing sand. Though their pessimism was slight, men told us that after the plundering of fruit and timber, this land would soon turn to desert. We walked on red sand, listened to the old-timers:

"before, there was never any of this damn dust here," discovered that the legacy of wealth would be a desert.

Sand that would turn this place that seemed fertile and forested from the air, into another pocket of poverty before the shoeshine boy became a grandfather. Before he knew one day of plenty.

Naturally, we did not say a word to anyone. How could we have dared to criticize progress? It would have been unpatriotic. But what kind of world is this world of ours, that leaves nothing but deserts and pockets of poverty in places the Good Lord did not forsake?

Before returning to my mountains, I dined once more in shirtsleeves, in the open air. I saw the shoeshine boy again. His hopes will never be fulfilled, I told myself. I have seen some of mine fulfilled, for I am fortunate: never to have known the "never" of this boy's life.

A "never" that is different from ours, because it is absolute.

∎∎∎ 87

Afterward, a few nights of reading confirmed the coming of the desert. Books no one reads.

And they are right.

For even if we read them, what could we do?

Nothing.

Before we have one day of plenty, progress will turn our land into an immense desert.

A future desert that prevents me from attending civic day parades.

∎∎∎ 88

At night, in front of the fire, drinking a beer, a painter with a goatee tells me of an unconfirmed rumor.

He says: Day doctors have discovered a fantastic life-prolonging drug. There is a gland at the base of the neck from which a fantastic liquid can be extracted. With it, the drug is made. Some doctors who live here are extracting the liquid from the necks of orphans, abandoned, uncared-for children, unwanted children, and they sell the liquid to their colleagues overseas.

Afterward, the children cannot raise their heads. Ever again. They lie there, in hospitals and dirty beds, before they die.

A few grams of this fantastic liquid are worth a fortune.

And the rich of the world can live for more than a hundred years.

The painter swears his story is the honest truth. What is to be done about such things?

Nothing.

It's the same thing that happens when you see the children in the Mississippi Delta and the shoeshine boy in Santa Cruz.

You look up to the starry sky, thank fate for not being one of those children, and order another beer.

■ ■ ■ 89

How can one, then, speak of ideologies?

The world is full of children who will never ever again be able to raise their heads. Machines poison the air and oceans and create deserts. Man, a wolf to man, is literally devouring the planet.

And in a pit that Nature's whim dug in between a sea, a frozen highland, and a desert, on a strip of land that cannot be seen from two thousand feet in the air, a few men deliver vociferous speeches in semi-deserted town squares, fire their weapons against their brothers, and content themselves with waging an absurd and eternal struggle. They wail, hate one another, and insult one another. Loot, murder, and destroy. Laugh, embrace, and forget the reason for their hatred and their laughter. They steal from one another because they seem not to have found other victims to rob or insult.

They invent and forget and reinvent their crimes and their innocence.

And those who can, escape to feast for two days on their slim pickings.

■ ■ ■ 90

But then, a truce, you flee down the road toward Palca, stop at the summit, from which the Father of All Mountains can be seen, you eat some bread, a piece of meat, a fruit. You touch the sky with your hands.

And there, beneath a cold sun and in the wind, far away from the steamy air of man's labors, every pore soaking up the beauty of this world, our world, you tell the last adventure of The Little Red Indian Girl and her struggle with the Big, Bad Balloon.

Children's laughter wafts in the wind.

Illimani bestows its pervasive and impassive beauty on you and you begin to weave hopes, because your hopes were half-asleep.

You say to yourself: this has to change. It must change. Some day . . .

The world is getting older, but it has a special magic: it dawns anew every day, virginal, newborn from the agony of the previous night. Not even innocence has perished yet: it floats over the valleys in children's laughter, finds a footpath where man has not yet trod.

This land, my land, is a source of happiness.

You say to yourself: How lucky I am, to have been born here . . .

Accepting the great absurdity, you are, for a moment, happy.

As I could not be anywhere else in the world.

NINE

■■■ 91

Carter states in today's newspaper that it would be desirable for Bolivia to gain access to the sea. Our Sea.

But, at the Luis Cesar exhibit, a fellow citizen of Carter's says:

"You people don't need the sea. You've lived without the sea for a hundred years. Why couldn't you live without it for a thousand?"

It is drizzling.

"Anyway, as a people, you have no sea consciousness."

The streets are sad, dark.

"You don't do anything to prove you have a sea consciousness, to show that you are aware of, feel, and suffer from the amputation."

Bonfires in the hills.

"Maybe you can be an inland people forever."

San Juan's night, the coldest night of the year, and it is raining.

"I've read the Admiral. He has proven that an air corridor can substitute for the sea,"—"Like the one in Berlin?" I jest—". . . and that would solve the whole problem."

The trouble with this business is that this man can get to Carter's ear through Vance. He works for him.

Far-off fireworks fade into a blanket blackness.

"I've been here for a year now. And all I've seen is one parade with flags and colored candles; all I've heard is hoarse shouting."

I would like to jump over the flames, like I used to. Have some punch, get close to the fire.

"The next day, all I saw were paper flags and colored candles littering the sidewalks."

Tomorrow, the garden will have ice sculptures.

"Are those your arguments for your claim to the sea? Are those all your arguments?"

It was better in the jungle. Big bonfires and our broad shadows over low clouds. The woods were thick with spirits.

"Shouting, little paper flags, colored candles. Emotion, pure emotion. Emotion—is that all?"

"No," I say, of course not.

A cup of hot *api,* a woman's hand, our joyful music: San Juan. Sometimes we danced all night.

"And I'll have you know, I've read a fair amount on the subject."

When will the Beast strike next?

"In fact, I've read everything I could find on the subject."

I look at him. He smiles: "Because I like this country. I've come to love this country."

When will we have our next Night of the Long Knives?

▪▪▪ 92

Two weeks later, after listening to a devastating speech given by Dr. Espada, he says, picking up where he'd left off:

". . . reclaim the sea with nothing but emotional shouting? Because emotionalism is all I've seen. All I've read is emotional or lyrical. Academic legalism. People with the memory of an elephant. In a certain sense, an admirable memory: 'At 6:15 on a sunny winter day, the Chancellor . . .'" He laughs. "The same detailed anecdotes retold a thousand times. But nothing more. Reasons, arguments? Figures? Statistics?"

I think: Faces? Hunger? Human beings?

He concludes: "Nothing but emotion."

"Our cause is just."

"That's what they all say, but they don't show it."

"Conquest does not legalize the spoils."

"Woe to the vanquished: Taiwan."

"Taiwan?"

"It's a situation that displeases me personally. But how can one ignore Mao's victory? Mao wins and Taiwan is China."

Woe to the vanquished.

"Force is an argument."

"One that we will never endorse."

"But Force plays a significant part in your daily lives. Force and Violence: absolute values. Are you telling me you don't have a local tradition of Force and Violence? The only rule of law here is Force. The only Law is the law that enforces Force . . . Not only here, but as you know, in many other places throughout the world."

I think: the Reign of the Beast.

The other night the sky was afire in pale hues, the other night, I remember. I wanted to jump over the fire, but . . . Jump like I did back then. Jump now, before the last night, the night of the long knives.

"If you people have learned anything . . ." He hesitates, but says it, ". . . you've learned to respect Force. Brute, blind, arbitrary Force. And it's been the case for over a century."

"The Reign of the Beast."

"Oh, by Tamayo. The sublime unknown."

Emotion, emotion. I think: what other argument do we need to prove our need for the Sea?

"It is not difficult to prove our rights. All published maps of the world, from the Spanish map forward, prove it."

"Oh, yes. I don't doubt your rights." He smiles politely into the distance. "What I question is your need for the sea. A hundred years is a hundred years."

"Well, do you know what a VW would cost me? You don't pay taxes, but I do. Counting customs charges . . ."

"Yes, well— but you, I mean, your people, are to blame for that."

"My dear sir, do you know how our miners live?"

"No. I've never been allowed to visit them."

"Do you know our miners' average life expectancy?"

"Forty-three, isn't it? It's unbelievable."

"But it's true."

"Unbelievable. Unbelievable, and deplorable."

"Do you know that we are the poorest country in the Americas, after Haiti?"

"A tragic history has its price."

"Tragic . . . Tragic and heroic, too. We have our '52. Our Revolution. And we will keep on fighting, alone. A people utterly alone in its agony."

"Oh, yes. Didn't Gonzalo Vasquez say that? I read it in Mariano Gumucio's work."

"It's the truth. It's the honest truth."

"Vasquez writes well. Gumucio writes well." He sighs and says, "Why doesn't someone do a book titled *The Road to the Sea*? Why doesn't someone show what the loss of your seaway has meant? Naturally, keeping lyricism and legalism out of it," he insists. "Facts. Simple, clear, obvious facts."

"We don't need those arguments. We have living proof. Proof that walks past every day. They live up that way. And anyone with eyes can see them. My people."

"Don't you see? There you go again, waxing lyrical."
He takes a sip; I do the same.

▪▪▪ 93

Three weeks later, after the opening night of "Sacar Viruta," he continues the same conversation.

"Politics in Latin America isn't very scientific, is it?"

I follow him: I wasn't talking about politics. I was talking about hunger, clothing, education. Hope.

"No one goes hungry in Bolivia. It's not that there isn't enough food, it's that people haven't learned to eat right. They eat spicy foods, food that makes the blood boil. For instance, no one drinks milk."

I take a sip. He does the same.

"The book you mention . . ."

"Yes."

". . . could be done without words. Images would suffice. Photographs. Engravings and photographs of the last hundred years."

"Really? So where are those engravings and photographs? How do you expect me to believe that a book of that kind hasn't been done in the last hundred years?"

"There are statistics, too. Figures. Sociological studies . . ."

"Really? Where? Why don't they walk along God's roads, everyone with a little Bible of the Sea in his pocket?"

"The book exists," I insist. "Maybe it's spread throughout many books, but it exists. We have never been able to forget our greatest tragedy. Not even for one day. Thousands have argued— and not purely emotionally—of our need for a seaway. And that is why, although we are weak, we are advancing our cause, the cause of Our Sea, with the strength of our arguments. The Bolivian Sea is a just cause, and some day it will be a reality."

"Force is a simple argument."

"Our need for the Sea is also simple."

"But where is it? I don't see this need."

You're annoying me, dear diplomat.

"It's in every face. In every child. And you don't have to be poor to feel it, touch it. Millions of our children have never seen the sea."

"Millions in Switzerland haven't, either."

"And many things are more expensive in La Paz than in New York, because we have no Sea."

"That's doubtful, to say the least. Think of your history."

"Yes, of course. The Reign of the Beast. But the loss of the Sea also caused the Reign of the Beast. Maybe if we had not lost the sea, it would have drastically reduced the days of the Beast among us."

"Maybe . . ."

People's hearty laughter bothers us a little.

"Tell me: how many children from Santa Cruz do you think have visited the Andean mines?"

I scratch my ear.

"It would be a good idea, don't you think?"

I think: there is no time for that. It will be too late.

"Show the scars of '79. The forever festering wounds inflicted in '79. All the wounds, not just the mines. Show the wounds to the people first, then to the world. Showing isn't the same thing as proving, but it would be a start, wouldn't it?"

"It's been done. Many books and eyewitness accounts . . ."

"Where are they? Where? . . . Anyway, what do books matter to a population that can't, or doesn't, read? Better yet, it could be set to music, don't you think? Teach about the missing sea through folk songs . . ."

The fox fires are bursting in the night and setting the clouds afire. The fox fires.

"The world is too preoccupied with its own dilemmas."

Word has it that the Long Knives will be flashing in two weeks. Word has it.

"Why not use the state propaganda machine for the job? USIS is USIS to us . . . It doesn't work for Nixon or Carter or Mondale . . ."

"You know why."

"Our hands are tied. We respect all people's wishes, and the sovereignty of all peoples."

"Yes," I say. "How long have you been a diplomat?"

"Oh, a long time."

"Well, then, you must know why."

▪▪▪ 94

"I'm a history buff," he says, starting in again after a Pepita Cocadu concert. "And our chats remind me of Hitler."

"What?"

"Yes, Hitler. The first thing Hitler did to create nationalism was to break the social barriers that restricted the youth. I saw boys from the countryside doing civil service work in cities, and city girls working in very small villages, on farms, all over Germany."

He takes a sip. I look at the sky.

"A few years later, they were ready to listen to him."

"This is the first time I've heard Hitler offered as an example for Bolivia."

"Of course, those kids were fanatics . . . And there was a wave of illegitimate births . . . But the youth served him well . . . They believed in him. They died on every front . . ."

He takes a sip. He looks at the wall. I take a sip. I look at him.

"The German youth had traveled all over Germany. They got to know Germany. They felt for Germany."

He sighs.

"And then they followed him."

"Well . . . To me, Hitler . . ."

"No . . . Of course not. He was a psychopath. But those kids died for him. For his Germany."

"We are part of the Americas. This isn't Broadway, but we are still in the Americas. We are citizens of Night, but we will see Day."

"Oh, yes. America is the land of hope and justice, isn't it?"

"I still believe that. We have suffered a long time but it will end. It has to . . ."

"You're a good man," he says. "I remember the Palestinians."

"What about them?"

"Well, the truth is that history can get depressing."

"Oh, yes! We know all about it. Have you read *Masamaclay*?"

"Very good, very good."

He gets up, peers through the curtain. The sky is afire. The people continue buzzing like bees. Martinis.

"No one can govern for long in the absence of dialogue."

"The Russians think our newspapers are foolish American luxuries. They don't understand the excesses that follow from being able to say what we think and live as we please, even if that means saying nothing but obscenities and living like dirty, naked savages in a desert commune."

He turns, finishes his drink.

"Excesses repulse me. But I accept them. They're the price I pay to read what I choose—whatever I damn please—and say what I like about movies the whole world makes. The price of dialogue is an excess of dialogue. Democracy."

"To my mind, it's a high price, but not too high. Unpleasant, but not overly unpleasant. It's a guarantee, nothing more than a guarantee."

"Good night."

"Where are you from?" I inquire.

"Dallas, Texas."

"Oh. Good night."

▪▪▪ 95

In Appendix D there is material for several *nivolas*.

I don't feel the least bit like trying. You will forgive me, won't you?

Thanks.

▪▪▪ 96

He was standing in front of the tailor's mirror, getting fitted while he sized himself up, beginning with the head.

Tonsured baldness: "Why don't you look after yourself? You'd look better if you took care of yourself." Because that liquid manure is good only to fool dolts. Let me be bald and leave me alone. In the end, who cares? Eyes, red streaks. In high altitudes, nearly everyone's eyes get red and then Dr. Pescador has to operate. "Why don't you go see Dr. Pescador? You ought to take better care of yourself." It annoys me. There are always fifteen people waiting their turns. I'll go some other time.

The nose: sinus infection. That was when you went to the coast and the dampness got to you. "Why don't you get an operation? You never take care of yourself." If my nose is going to get stretched out so I look like a clown, like Don Raul, I'd rather leave it the way it is, you know.

The teeth: "You have a cavity there. Why don't you go to the dentist and get it filled? Take care of yourself, please." He puts in cotton wads. He takes out cotton wads. The cotton wads go in and out for months on end. I have no time these days. Besides, it doesn't hurt. I'll go. I'll go later, honey. That does it for the head.

Chest: does it hurt anywhere? No. Cheer up: you'll live to be as old as Grandpa, into your seventies.

Belly: bulging a bit, my man. You drink too much. The Liver, yes, with a capital L. It will hold out. It doesn't hurt. Gas on occasion. Indigestion? Never. My stomach is consistent, like a clock. "Why don't . . . ?" Honest, it's nothing serious. Kidneys? Fine. Penis: Doctor, it was cut in El Callao. Serious injury. A jealous husband. Yes, but does it hurt? No, it's just that—well, it always points north-northwest, no matter what the weather. But does it hurt? No, doctor, it doesn't. Good. Sex? A few times a week. Children? Three. Others? Yes, thank you. You're welcome. Knees, tending to knock-kneed, diet . . . ? Feet? An annoying corn, yes. Anything else? No, nothing.

Fine: come back next week to try it on, all right? the tailor says.

A lot of whisk, he thinks.

What time? he asks.

He hears: at five.

Fine, he says, good-bye.

He hears: good day now.

Man in the mirror: man, wolf to man.

Ha.

Howl.

▪▪▪ 97

Flaco: No one silenced you . . . The trouble is that, in the bourgeois life you lead, nothing new happens. What could you tell?

"I have a few ideas."

Flaco: So, work, then.

"I am. I'm working on it."

Flaco: Ha.

"But I am. I'll show you sometime."

Flaco: How does that story go, the one about Anita Ana?

"I'll treat you to coffee."

▪▪▪ 98

Eleven years earlier, a Chilean, an Italian, an Arab, a Brazilian, a Yankee, and I myself were crossing the eternity of plenty in a bottle green van.

It's called the Midwest.

Hogs the size of elephants, ears of corn the size of two watermelons, silos as big as mountains, highways across the fruited plain from horizon to horizon, like knife incisions on the flat face of the planet.

From six in the morning until eleven at night.

Hogs, corn, silos, highway.

Then, at midday, we got hungry.

We entered a little village invented by Tennessee Williams.

Let's have lunch, we said.

We had lunch: a bowl of broth fit for tuberculosis patients. No meat today. Soda: The formidable empire of Coca-Cola. Tea.

The campesinos—farmers, as peasants are known there—looked at us suspiciously, like *aymarás*. Pale, colorless eyes, pupils made of ice.

Elvis Presley moaned on the jukebox.

We left as hungry as we had been when we went in.

This poor country has never heard of *jallpahuaica*. Or *aji*.

They eat out of obligation.

Not much, because it is God's will.

And they work from sunup to sundown.

They are healthy as bulls, strong as oxen. They pray in church on Sundays.

God rewarded them.

By then I had the cavity in my molar.

I still have it, eleven years later.

Man is wolf to man: leave my molar alone.

And let them keep their sickly soup with six grains of corn per portion.

That one does not even know he is exploited.

We left to see the world, flying happily down the highway.

A flat world that God sowed with plenty.

Fish-eyed, farmer, who never tried to talk to me.

To travel so far, just to remember *jallpahuaica*.

If man must somehow take his own measure, his measure must be in his ability to absorb the absurd.

Infinite ability.

Like Martians, we disappeared into the night.

▪▪▪ 99

But I would go back, just to see the highways.

It is worth the trip, just for the highways.

Let your feet take a rest; wheels abound. You can cross the world in a comfortable seat. I know of no other country where a person can be so free.

You can fly, jump, roll, dash about, die free.

No one has grandparents: everyone is what he seems.

To move is to live; to stop is to die.

There is no such thing as friends, only acquaintances. There are no secrets, only strangers. There are no lies: lying is a waste of time because no one listens to what anyone says. There are no mysteries, only airplanes. There are no cities, only concrete monsters glowering at dusk through a billion eyes. And we are all alone, that is why we talk in bars. What does it matter? We will never see each other again. We can be sincere because it is free.

America, America of my oppressors, you made me love you.

It is night time and I am traveling in a Greyhound.

Where am I going? I don't remember. Why am I going? I don't know. Is it worth it? Who knows.

I know where I am: in America.

Only in America could something like this happen to me.

Eleven years ago, I was in the Day.

I was young and felt happy.

Today, I am fading into Night.

I am no longer young.

And, smoking, I look at the stars twinkle, so many of them twinkling.

I do not find what I deserve, only what I am.

■■■ 100

Let's nivolize; let's nivolize.

The Return:

An irate God resides in these altitudes. All very lovely, all very pleasant from a plane, everything pretty, why deny it. Latin America, folklore, exoticism, jungle, beauty, vastness, a monstrous Titanic animal whose spine is the snow-capped Andes and whose claws are sunk deep in the rocks of the Amazon . . . But day begins to break and we fly home, higher and higher, and suddenly, great heavens: Mother Nature is the talking biped's enemy, and everything becomes hostile, sprawling, threatening, huge, aggressive, frozen, fearsome, even to the naked inhabitants of these lands.

The Sacred Lake: with a puff, the belly of the metal

fish scores your impassive face, blue mirror of the pale sky, leaving our steam-lined trail across its surface. Looking out the window now makes you feel as though a little magic wand just turned you into a black ant. It makes you fear God, a God who seems capricious and wrathful. In other words: By Jupiter! And wouldn't it be better in the Caribbean?

The basin where my city, my vertical city, sits, does not merely seem strange, it looks like the footprint a giant left in a crevice in the earth. And behind it, mountains. And beyond that, the jungle. And beyond that? *Madre mía,* I feel Lilliputian. Insect-sized. Gonococcus. Fish piss in a petrified sea. Terrible.

Who lives here? asks Rosemary, Thomas's daughter. He is an executive for Gulf.

Daddy says: Big, three-eyed beasts with hemispheric bellies of ferocious proportions, whose teats hang down as if in tribute to a fertile mother; their feet have twelve toes and their hands, twelve fingers; their heads are hollow like the moon, their souls, sacrificed to the low passions of the black angel Pepin Ferulero!

Rosemary: Oh, maybe we'd better go on to Asunción.

Daddy says: No, that's not true, those are tall tales. The people who live here are people like anyone else, they have two feet, arms, eyes, ten fingers and toes, a stomach, children, grandchildren, installment payments, dreams of owning their own homes.

Rosemary: Oh, goodie. Let's go on to Asunción.

Daddy: I can't; business is business.

Rosemary: Shit!

But here we go, Rosemary: we are descending onto the bloody bald spot of the highland, half-heartedly fighting the winds that whistle past, making the metal plates tremble with a mysterious death rattle. Peoples' hands are sweating; prayers are being recited in low voices of intense concentration; for a few minutes, the aisles are a temple of fear. The engines thunder in reverse as they try gearing down to brake, inches away from tragedy, before the end of the longest runway in the world. It comes to a stop, but with technology straining to the last screw.

The plane seems relieved as the people exhale. The air is so thin it is practically nonexistent. Still tensed, the plane quiets down, then struts in glee, like someone who has gotten his way. The wind blows with all its might, forces open the airtight doors, mocks the air conditioner, lifts the stewardess's Hawaiian-style skirt—long, stylized legs, vision of dense and impossible metropolis—whooshingly whips around the cabin and delivers a thudding, icy hammer blow to the chests of those in attendance.

Greetings, son; welcome. A fat gringo with a cherubic smile suddenly turns purple in the face. His smile becomes grotesque and toothy as his legs shake beneath the seat and he foams at the mouth.

"Oxygen!"

There he goes. Welcome. Another second and he would have been in the bone pile. Before he could see a thing and after thirty years as a used car salesman. Poor guy. But there, he's breathing now. The stewardess doesn't say a word. "There's always one, every landing—that's if we're lucky," dumb, bearded Bobby Johnson says insolently. He's with a skinny blond marijuana smoker and with his Texan father. Erp, says the blond, and there she goes, under the seat.

But we have arrived. Like Columbus on the deck of his boat, I look out from the top of the stairway and, consciously or unconsciously, bow my head respectfully before the silent god who rules this world, my world: glorious Illimani, Mother and Father of Mountains, the Immortal Never Created, Lord of Titans, Heroes, and Gods, I salute you. A not-quite Ph.D. salutes you. Father, here

I am. I have returned. Coughing, feverish, exhausted, an amputated failure chattering in English, I have returned. Father, here I am. Hip, hip, hurrah! Father, your son, suffering from anguish, exhaustion, and death rattles, is here. So walk, you idiot, it's freezing out.

There's Julio. Hi, Julio! Daddy isn't here. He couldn't come: an incident. Died twenty years ago. Unavoidable prior commitment, son. There, now. These things happen.

Hey, brother! Son of a gun, he grew so tall he looks like a tree. And who are all these people? Familiar faces. God help me match the names to the faces, now don't put your foot in your mouth, okay?

TEN

▪▪▪ 101

And so, you ask: which is our Revolution?

What's the matter: do you smell here a mockery made of a hundred tricks perpetrated at word-point and on the cutting edge of words? Do you demand: give us something solid, man, something we can sink our teeth in?

The Revolution is to fold our hands.

To fold our hands, literally.

To fold our hands day and night.

Refusing instead of striving.

Giving instead of grabbing—nothing original here.

Listening and understanding instead of demanding.

Apprehending that we are all equal, all mestizos with no place in the sun.

Knowing that we are alone, mestizos, all alone against the world.

Grasping our unavoidable solitude.

Accepting our struggle, ours, and against all—all, not only the sea thieves.

But, to fold our hands.

To fold our hands against the murderous hot lead fired by our brothers against us.

To fold our hands against the hate fired by the Beast,

when he hollers for a thousand days: "Communist, radical, atheist!"

But for one thousand days we will have to fold our hands.

Not a glance in our eyes. Not moving one finger. Not milling another grain. Not starting another engine. Not talking to anyone. Not a blink, a murmur, a moan, however slight.

To paralyze the earth.

Not sowing. Not harvesting. Not manufacturing. Not mining. Not burning minerals. Not eating nor breathing.

Until they learn. Until they know that we'd rather choose death in our own way than life as we are forced to live it.

To fold our hands and to die, to conquer life.

Not hating. Looking piteously upon our murderers. Not sneering. Looking patiently upon the Beast, for patience will still be possible.

To let ourselves be killed.

But folding our hands. Never again returning to the mine. Never again opening the factory. Never saying another word. To fold our hands until we see them die as we keep our hands folded.

They will die because there will be no bread, our bread, to feed their children. There will be no heat, no tomorrow, no hope for them or the Beast. Then they will know that they were beaten without hate, without blame, without a word of scorn.

How will they tire their triggers on our chests.

How will they excite their sick hatred on our skin.

How will they tire of torturing, how will they exhaust their scientific ability to annihilate us. And how slowly, how very slowly, will they learn, these brothers of ours who murdered us for a century and a half, that they will be defeated, that they always were defeated.

It will be the Night of our Blood.

This handful of killers with empty past and empty future, these ferocious animals who somehow found a place in our guts, will see that they cannot defeat us, that they never defeated us, that their glorious victories were mindless massacres allowed by our immortality, our greatness.

How will they marvel at our will to give our blood.

How will they learn that they can bathe in our blood, our innocent blood, until they drown, and how will they learn, in terror, that there will be more deaths, more victims, more children and men and women and old people they will have to sacrifice to their vain attempts to perpetuate their lies.

This will be a long Night of Blood.

But not as long as this agony, this lasting suffering that lasts still.

It will have a meaning.

They will read this meaning in our eyes at the very moment when they murder us. They will feel it in their skin when their crime-weary hands tremble. They will know it in their souls when they face the new terror of the emptiness to which we will sentence them.

Because one day, only one day when we can call the sun our own, is worth more than a hundred and fifty years of orphanage, of an alien world, of a land ravaged by our sacrifice, of our children's, born to be slaves, of ourselves, ourselves, never able to live with bread and dignity.

Look here, I say, how easy: there's no need to read any books. It is not necessary to know anything. We don't need to believe in anything.

We need only appeal to our consciences.

To respect ourselves.

To decide we are men, not beasts.

And then . . . to fold our hands.

Fold our hands until the day we are waiting for actually dawns.

That Day.

To keep our hands folded until that Day arrives.

Though the world's hatred be hurled at us. Though murderers flood the horizons with our blood. Though the Beast belch, choke on our bones. And though the sun, terrified, decides to die out.

Though they scatter our ashes throughout the universe.

And even though our remembrance be vanished forever.

This is how we must respect ourselves.

This is how we must love our right to be human.

This is how we must seek our freedom.

And this is how we must love ourselves. . . . We, who know that we do not kill, hate, or live off the sacrifices of others.

This is our Revolution.

It is the conquest of our entity.

It is leaving the tribe behind and beginning to found a nation.

It is setting a Day in which we begin to be what we ought to be.

Rejecting the century and a half during which we never were what we must be.

Rejecting it outright. With a single stroke. Rejecting it forever.

Doing nothing but folding our hands.

Dying, to conquer life.

Being murdered to let a new Day dawn for those who will follow. A Day without dark memories. A Day without false promises, cowardice, hollow words, a Day without a thousand minor indignities.

The Day of our People.

For it is true: the People are immortal and the Beast will perish.

It is true: the Beast dies facing our silent scorn.

The Beast will die as shadows die when the sun is born.

And our Night of Blood shall be sad.

For our father shall betray us, our children, our brothers, our mother shall betray us.

They shall speak beautiful words. They shall offer peace and individual satiation in exchange for our kinsmen's hunger, of new sacrifices to be made by our mestizos with no place under heaven.

But we must deny these voices, these lies and promises, our own hopes, our need for finding individual fulfillment and individual freedom and contentment at long last.

We must refuse to unfold our hands until we reach our Day.

And we must keep our hands folded.

For the Day will come, and the fewer traitors among us, the sooner it will come. And the more willingly we allow the blood to flow over our folded hands, the sooner will it arrive. And the more among us who can keep our hands folded without fear of dying, the sooner it will arrive.

The Beast will disappear the way a bad dream recedes. Blood will flow like rainwater in a downpour, it is true, but then we will see the Day beginning. It will be a long Day.

It will be Our Day.

Our hands will touch the Andes and our feet will bathe in the sea.

Our Sea.

This is, Brothers and Sisters, the Revolution.

To fold our hands.

To paralyze the earth.

With our hands folded.

Everybody.

Everybody, Brothers and Sisters, everybody, until Our Day dawns.

And not before it dawns.

Not one second, one death, one tear, one victim before it dawns.

That is all there is to it, Brothers and Sisters.

Peoples who are, waged this battle and won.

Peoples who never were, never fought it, never perceived it.

If we have the will to be, we must fold our hands.

Now.

▪▪▪ 102

But how, you will ask, to let them kill us as if we were animals?

But what are you saying, you will murmur, to let them murder us without even wielding a stone?

But it is impossible, you will swear; how can we allow them to destroy our seed, without one roar of wrath?

But what are we, you will protest, what: poor little animals, despicable beings, things with no face, no God, no light?

Brothers and Sisters, with your hands on your hearts now:

What are we?

What are we, now?

▪▪▪ 103

What, then, can we possibly hope for, we who have chosen to build a future on the innocent blood of the weakest among us?

What are we building on this tradition of ours made of murdering, burning, destroying, torturing the saddest among us? What can we say about our Day when there is no other vision than this tireless labor of those whose sacrifices put bread on our tables?

On which blood brotherhood can we found the day of

our replevies when we count only one victory, this victory over our brothers and, among them, the naked, the sick, the loneliest?

With what vision can we dream a future, when our memories are drowned in a present pierced by lies, vileness, shameful ambitions grounded on thousands of tombs no one remembers?

How can we create a hope of unity when brother murders brother, father lies to child, child steals from father, and mother refuses herself to all?

How can we think of hope, let alone name it, when we reject a confession of our sorrows?

What curse is this, which forces us to kill our own blood to see a piece of bread on our table?

And what kind of table is that, which can accept and welcome such bread?

How can we allow this eternal, black, frozen, sad Night that endures, endures still and seems to endure forever, and not allow our Day, just one Day, but truly ours, our Day?

What monstrous anger has been set afire in us to perpetuate the torture and suffering of our Brothers and Sisters?

From whence this destiny?

How can we break it?

How can we change it?

How can we tear these shadows so we can finally give to those who follow a new dawn, a dawn our consciences demand?

By folding our hands.

Today.

▪▪▪ 104

For it is true that the Night of our Blood is already upon us.

And this Night of our Blood is meaningless because not everyone is taking part in it.

Some preach of plenty, patting their bellies.

And they are satisfied.

And they yell: "Monster!" to the man in anguish, the man whose anguish still endures.

But they are few.

They are the Beast.

The blind Beast.

The Beast who will perish only when we fold our hands.

The Beast who is alive because we do not dare create our Day. A Day requiring nothing, neither dreams nor promises, nor hopes. A Day requiring neither effort nor heroic sacrifices, nor shouting in town squares.

A Day that lies waiting to be born, waiting for us to fold our hands.

Everyone.

Until we see it dawning.

It's that easy.

And that difficult.

It's that simple.

And that horrendous.

For, Brothers and Sisters, there is no other way, there is no other way.

The Day will come.

Then . . .

■■■ 105

Let us not forget, Brothers and Sisters, that we, we immortals, are truly the masters of that "Then . . ."

Because we are a million faces.

A million sets of arms.

A million lives.

And we can wait for that "Then . . .", whereas the Beast cannot wait.

Tomorrow belongs to us.

So long as we can kill this Today, without hatred or rancor, merely by searching our conscience.

This terrible Today made of our eternal agony.

■■■ 106

Flaco: You have nothing left to say. What do you expect, after twelve years of bourgeois life? Not a peep.

But I do, of course I do. It is all waiting to be done in this country. Waiting to be said. And thought. Every day is . . .

Flaco: You don't have the vaguest memory of your ideals . . . All you want is a house, a car, a salary, and a trip to Los Yungas on Sundays.

No, not really. I keep reading, I read more and more. I write sometimes, too, just a bit . . .

Flaco: What about Anita? How does the story go?

Bolivians do not read Bolivian books because Bolivian authors do not write the right kinds of books, the kinds we need . . .

Flaco: Sure! And you, of course, know what they ought to write . . .

No. But it is still going round and round in my head like a dog chasing its tail.

Flaco: Sure, sure. Forget your tail for a minute. How does the story about Ana go?

Which one?

Flaco: Anita Ana.

Better yet, I'll treat you to coffee.

■■■ 107

Skinny Ms. Beatriz, wearing her intellectual glasses: But, didn't you say before: "Action. Folding our hands is complicity"?

Yes, I did, but . . .

Serious Ms. Beatriz, tireless student of journalism: Did you or didn't you?

Yes, but . . .

Beatriz, strict mother of three: You are contradicting yourself.

No, I'm not.

Sad Ms. Beatriz, a misunderstood chatterbox: Oh, yes you are.

I said that before, because I believed that we would win by those means, but I was mistaken. And winning is all.

Beautiful Ms. Beatriz, woman of intense passions: You said it, you said it, you said it. You are contradicting yourself. It is not consistent, not at all.

I was seven years younger . . .

Julio: Minutiae.

I do not contradict myself . . . I mean, yes, I do contradict myself. You see . . . I . . .

Lovely Ms. Beatriz, biting her pencil: Aha!

Julio: It is not consistent.

When I said that, when I said that folding your hands was complicity, I thought that we could win by violent means. That both battle and victory were possible. That our enemies' blood would wash away a century and a half of . . .

Sweet Ms. Beatriz, smiling sadly: Yet, now . . .

Now . . . Now I see that it's impossible. Warfare is a road that is closed to us. It is hopeless. It would only perpetuate the suffering that endures so long and endures still.

Cruel Ms. Beatriz: So . . . now what?

Now . . . now I see that our satrapy has been cursed by men of action . . . I think that our passivity, the deliberate indifference of the average poor, exploited man is the only way to open a vista somewhere . . . I think that there will be a struggle, but that it will be a passive one, that we will have to bare our chests to the blaze of bullets, that it is enough to simply fold one's hands . . .

Logical Ms. Beatriz: Folding one's hands equals complicity.

Yes . . . before. But not anymore. Now we know that there is only one way to overcome the Beast: choke him with our death. Paralyze the world: the Beast's world, not our world . . .

Julio: It's just what I say: Minutiae.

Cold Ms. Beatriz: You are contradicting yourself.

But no: listen . . .

Tired Ms. Beatriz: What now? Go ahead.

Before, I thought we could win through violence. But we cannot. It's impossible: there are peoples who are Corsairs and there are peoples who are shepherds. Only one way remains: to bare one's chest and paralyze the world, this world that belongs to others.

Ms. Beatriz: You mean . . .

I mean that the time has come to toll the death of ideologies.

Julio: Minutiae! . . . Revolution: a new, original way of doing things. Re-evolution is out of the question. It is easier to criticize a given state of affairs than to create a different, better state of affairs. You are a dilettante: you speak simplistically, disregard too many things . . .

Flaco: You drink too much.

No: I know that logic would impel us to accept this as the best of all possible worlds, but my heart tells me it isn't: there is too much suffering. There must be another way . . . and not through violence: after all, Christianity . . .

Triumphant Ms. Beatriz: Hey!

Julio: Ha!

Folding your hands . . . I tell you, that is all it will take. Winning—if we cannot win by action, win by inaction: folding your hands to strangle the world, their world.

After all, what can they do without us? We produce for them, consume for them . . . But: what would they do in an empty world?

Cold Ms. Beatriz: You are contradicting yourself.

Julio: You are splitting hairs.

But . . . this world is corrupt! There must be an alternative . . .

Sad Ms. Beatriz: You are not being coherent, either.

Julio: The world is what it is and will be what it will be. Fold our hands!

She: You drink too much.

Julio: You are not being coherent.

Flaco: Your "democracy" is on its way out . . .

She: You drink a lot . . .

But, it is simple . . . the first voice is mine, the second belongs to all of us.

She: You drink too much. Don't you remember what I told you? You don't sleep enough, or soundly enough. Couldn't you cut down on your smoking? Why don't you go to bed early one of these nights? You have bags under your eyes . . .

Flaco: You contradict yourself; you contradict yourself . . .

It's elementary: for me, this talking biped, the Beast is immortal; for my Great Family the Beast is born of our petty stupidity, our ignorance, our cowardice . . . The People are immortal, the People . . . Flaco.

Flaco: You are contradicting yourself again.

Julio: You are splitting hairs.

She: Can't you stop drinking? It's bad for you . . .

Oh, damn it, how hard the siren song is, isn't it.

▪▪▪ 108

She: (awakening all of a sudden) How much longer will you be?

Me: Just a little while longer . . . Go back to sleep.
She: I can't . . . Come to bed.
Me: I can't stop now. A little longer, okay?
She: Hurry up and finish.
Me: In a minute.
She:

▪▪▪ 109

The Beast: Traitor! Let him rot!
   Me: No, please, this is only fiction.
   The Beast: Ha!
   Me: Even if it's fiction, it's my duty . . .
   The Beast: What is "fiction"?

▪▪▪ 110

The moon is shining and soon it will be day.

Everything is illuminated in that white, thin air that allows us to see eternities.

The mountains shine, a brilliant blue, forever someone else's, outline of clouds and snow.

Lights blink forlornly on the hilltops. Some are flickering out.

I walk alone, hands in my coat, the cold air biting my face.

Day will dawn, and once again I have been wandering aimlessly along the byways of my city.

Once again, I have paused before every shadow, every sorrow, every desperate cry, every body on the pavement, every pained groan, every pair of dark, sad eyes, plumbing their mysteries, searching others' eyes, others like me, whose eyes are feverish because they have lost the trail.

The street sweepers, bent over, mumble indistinctly to themselves as their brooms lick the avenues.

Walking slowly, gingerly touching every tree and wall, every person, dead or alive, watching the grayness grow brighter in the sunlight, squinting from the bright, intense colors of the fruit in the makeshift market that opens with a splash of sun in the cool morning, walking under the cloth tents among the fresh smells of the earth, I know: it could not be otherwise. I could not have been another. There are no roads other than my roads.

It is only here that there has been and will be room for me.

I must exhaust my experience, though I know not to what end.

I read it in everyone's eyes as I walk home. When all is said and done, this must be what weariness is.

Our weariness.

ELEVEN

▪▪▪ 111

By the third night I got fatalistic and felt strangely indifferent; I am under the thumb of the Beast, I thought, and there is nothing I can do about it. I cannot rebel, because they would beat me to death; I cannot take my own life, for that would give them satisfaction, and besides, if I did, it would be a coward's death. What would it feel like to have a father who was a coward?

But I will get out of here, I told myself, unconvinced. I don't know how, but I will. Try to sleep a little.

Out in the yard the Beast was yelling. He was banging chains against the cell bars, a lovesick drunkard. He was playing with his six-shooter. From time to time, he shouted:

"Gonzalez, José!"

"Here!"

"Get your things and step out!"

The Reign of the Beast roars.

And we, the cage-dwellers, are nobodies.

One shouts: *Viva la Patria*!

The Beast replies: *Viva*!

Stupid . . .

Thus, in ataraxy, the third day ended.

You: Traitor! One doesn't say these things out loud!

▪▪▪ 112

Oh, what fear the Beast instills!

Yet, where does this fear come from? In the final analysis, if this world is hell, one must be grateful to the Beast for the passage to infinity. Naturally, he has no pity: he kicks stomachs until they burst, fills lungs with water, beats genitals until they are deformed, invents new, more ingenious ways of delivering our passports to nowhere; he hurts and harms relatives, friends, and acquaintances.

The weapon he uses is terror, and he uses it skillfully. The delicate art of torture has reached exceptional heights. The Beast knows, Dictum One: "We Beasts are few—only a handful; the fewer we are, the more terror we must spread." It is only by terrorizing everyone that the Beast remains strong.

But it is not only that. His terror can prevent a great temptation: since he cannot accompany us beyond death, we can always tempt death, and the Beast knows it. That is why, among his other amazing instruments, is the legacy this century's scientists have left us: he breaks the prisoners' minds and disrupts space and time; thus does he create the absurdity of his hatred. He so convincingly pretends to hate that he learns to hate at will. The Beast's magnificent stupidity, divine imbecility, meaningless hate is his most potent weapon. He classes us all as enemies, ascribes to us his own desire to annihilate his foes, both real and imagined, and then he declares war on us without reason or motive, without pity and without any rules whatsoever.

It is his animal and superhuman stupidity that enables him to live. This primal, primitive brutality that has been successfully manufactured by advanced technology and with sophisticated experimentation, taught and studied according to infallible methodology and applied systematically, routinely: this wonderful technique for destroying one's brethren, combined with his intense rage, is what creates the Beast's brand of terror.

The simple fact that the Beast exists, that he carries out his tasks with the dedication and skill of a country doctor, that he seems, or actually is, just like the rest of us because after an interminably long session of torture he can go home and have lunch with his children—confounds common understanding; the challenge to the imagination and this violent awakening is what causes our greatest terror. Whereas reading seemed to indicate that before it ends, this century would produce another Beethoven, instead this century has spawned the Dynasty of the Beast, a beast created in the most advanced laboratories; instead we have Michelangelo's successor, a much-improved Torquemada: he has a thousand faces, a thousand lives, skin of every color, speaks every language, and will inherit the Universe.

For man's son, denial of dignity is another source of terror: forty years' worth of books, paintings, melodies, and abstractions can dissolve in a blink of the Beast's eye peering into a cell: You are nothing, he declares, you have always been nothing; for if the Beast exists, the Beast is all that ever existed. The road toward utopia was not a possibility, then; it was a myth. It was merely a thin disguise . . . This is the true terror the Beast spreads: the conviction that we are all Beasts like him. That we all identify with him. That I have lived forty years of lies, and the species has lived forty centuries of fallacies, of fiction. A Mozart recording, a book by Goethe, "peace on earth," all lies.

Everything begins in the Beast, everything ends in the Beast: bite your dust.

In this century of uranium, take your pick: bread without dignity, animal systole and diastole—your life; or twenty hours of torture and your death.

The price tag on your life is your dignity: pay up and live.

If you don't pay, you die.

And this, my stupid friend, is the whole story.

But, what about famous, prestigious, powerful people? They all paid their tithe.

But, what about honest, hardworking, heroic people? They lie in unmarked, forgotten graves.

And this is the world where I have sentenced my children to live?

Yes.

Someone: . . . the nation is in great danger. I ask all citizens to be prepared to lay down their lives, if necessary, to face the dangers and threats to our nation's sovereignty.

Me: What a cross I leave them to bear . . .

Someone else: You always have the lie . . . Serve it!

Someone else: Long may it live!

Yet another: Long Live the Lie!

I have not lived long: I have not yet learned to serve the Lie . . .

The Beast: Well, get over here: take him to the Office of National Security!

This, my stupid friend, is the whole story.

▪▪▪ 113

She: You can never talk to anyone. You can never be happy. We have no friends, we never go out, everything boils down to work and troubles. Sorrow . . . and what's more, you drink.

Me: Close the door.

A young, intelligent television reporter: Why don't you write another book? Are you afraid of the critics?

Me: No, I'm not afraid of the critics, but of the Beast . . .

The television reporter: I don't understand . . .

Me: Lucky for you.

Me: I am dead.

Me: Yes, and alone.

Me: But they still need you.

Me: Yes.

Me: You will have to last another twenty years . . .

Me: Yes.

Me: So what are you going to do about it?

Me: Cheers!

▪▪▪ 114

Had I been born in another place it would have been possible to sit in a cathedral and be busy writing dialogues in order to live in Barcelona and write more little pieces for Patiño's magazine.

Had I looked at the world from a different angle, I might have caught a chance to shut myself in a library for half a lifetime, to go blind and then deliver speeches at conferences in Indiana.

Had I been conceived at some other point on the horizon, let's say in a place without mountains, chances are I might have got inspired in order to end up being a professor in New Jersey, where I would have held forth on the writers from this lacerated continent.

Had I been higher-born—more dough, that is—I would have had time at my disposal, to leave in order to then grab a different passport and open a hot dog stand in Chicago.

Had I been born cleverer—that is, a thief—I would have taken advantage of local opportunity to stuff my pockets: what are five years of nervous pacing during the Dance of the Assassins in exchange for forty thousand dollars, the amount one needs (so they tell me) to get a visa and live happily ever after somewhere else?

Had I been born less clever—that is, a hit man—there would have been ample chances to earn a few years with a satisfied belly by torturing and killing.

Had I been born a soccer fan instead of being, from an early age, so irresponsibly, fatally, irreversibly addicted to the printed word, the contentment of simple souls could have been mine: a few years of ignorance and then the cemetery.

Had I been born without this stupid weakness of taking some words seriously, chances are I would have taken things lightly, opting to follow fashion; disdain posterity; behold, the road to a peaceful life as a public servant.

Had I been born near a rifle rather than near a library, I would have had more opportunities to become a pirate, a thief, and a businessman. It would have been sufficient to praise, clap on cue, sell my writing, even if mediocre.

Had I accepted the transparent truths that not all men are created equal, that the masses are but a pretext for individuals with king-sized ambitions, that there is no life other than this one, no other way of life, our crazy lottery game, that no one, not a soul, can take from you what you ate and drank and caught and burned; I would have had other roads to travel, other carrots to chase.

Had I been born in another place, at another time, under another star . . .

Someone else.

But since things do not happen that way and never will, the question: "What shall I do with myself now?" hangs over me every day, every minute, every second.

Hangs there, naturally, with no answer.

One's anguish increases when one realizes that, out of every five people one passes on the street, four are in the same situation, asking themselves the same unanswered question.

The fifth, my friend, is the Beast.

From the Rio Grande to Cape Horn.

But you will have to last another twenty years.

Then, of course, the Countryside, the Mine, the City are still there. If someone wrote the Great Novel of the Countryside . . . the Great Novel of the Mine . . . The Great Urban Novel . . . that somebody could solve his problems: his life would have a meaning.

Why don't we write the Great Novel of the Countryside?

Well, because there never was a Great Countryside Story. All we have had were little country stories told by little country storytellers about the little lives of the little inhabitants of the countryside.

And besides that, because it is a very boring story.

It is the same story from Cape Horn to the Rio Grande.

And it is not populated by great men, but by little men. Losers, the defeated, men annihilated by their smallness. Men whose victories were always written against their own peoples, those innocent, naked, defenseless peoples. Men who repeated the same story time and time again, from the day Pedrarias set foot in the New World.

Never could a Great Story be written if all its characters were dwarfs. Dwarfs are good characters for dwarf stories only.

Bolívar, Sucre, San Martín, Martí?

Martians, that's who they were: Martians. Mutants.

"But wouldn't they be good models for . . ."

Now? At the dawn of the twenty-first century? When our species is looking to the stars and preparing for the Great Leap?

Oh, no. The thing is, one hundred and fifty years of stupidity exacts its price, my friend.

That is why some men sit in cathedrals to write dialogues: to go off to live in Barcelona, where it is much easier to navigate in social circles by means of clever, artful language . . . That is why other men spend half their lives shut in dark libraries and do not come out until the day they go blind: it is always a very human destiny to give speeches to youngsters near and far on the tragedies one could never see clearly, or weakly, for that matter. That is why . . .

Night, the desperation of Night, the mute distress of those who linger in Night, is fine material for spinning tales of magic realism, for artfully describing the desperate tantrums of our demi-men—where, oh where is the biography of Vallejo?—and for fleeing, leaving Night behind by going off on other tangents.

But, yes, we know: Had I been born under another sky, if other horizons, etc., etc.

At this moment, I ask myself: Where is the magic realism of the Vietnamese? Where, the brilliant history of their Novel over the last quarter-century? Where are their bards, orators, and writers? Where?

No one will construe these lost lines as criticism, will he? How obvious it is that the gods were egotists when it came to me; they made me a simpleton and a stutterer . . . When all is said and done, I am crushed by the fable about throwing the first stone . . .

▪▪▪ 115

I must avow: I am no better than any other man born under this sky. I must state: I am worthless compared with these men who provide me with a pretext for chasing my carrot. I must repeat, so as to make it clear: nothing makes me different from any other native of Night.

Only the dimensions of my betrayal.

Others' betrayals pulled them out of Night.

They went to Barcelona, to Indiana, to New Jersey, to "Paris, France."

Mine did not suffice: here I am, timid as the rest, fettered to my Great Cell.

For, another silenced aspect of the truth: for more than a century, people have been fleeing Night.

Only the least fortunate have remained behind.

The others have left: some, through Letters; others, through Money; still others, through Politics.

And even others, by swimming to Australia.

Only we subhumans have remained here.

We do not have enough coins to leave.

Those old coins that never lose their value.

Those coins, I believe, that the ancients called "talents."

And that is how I know: my talents are not enough.

I can use mine only to do what all do: while away my life amidst trivialities and sadness in this satrapy.

▪▪▪ 116

And, nevertheless, I do not know whether it is the least bit noticeable: I have not yet betrayed myself.

I contradict myself sometimes, because things themselves are contradictory.

But, don't tell anyone: I do not lie to myself.

To myself, I do not lie.

I know what is there for me.

Alone, I want for it.

I fret, get drunk, insult everyone, act like a pig. I cry at night, consider the possibilities of being just a trifle satisfied with myself someday, know them too scarce; I shout, spit, drink, insult people, I laugh at myself, walk these streets as though a dagger were piercing my heart—and it is—I screech, make my family and strangers suffer.

I walk about, frustrated, barely able to eke out a living.

But I do not lie to myself.

I see what I see, hear what I hear, feel what I feel.

And when I can, I say so.

Say it exactly as I see it, hear it, and feel it.

And even, if I can, I publish it.

Granted, it's mediocre; not prize-winning material, of course.

Boring, like the whole Great Story, but genuine.

Mine.

Lovingly tendered to My Family. Humbly tendered and with every wish to be of service.

Asking nothing in return; perhaps for a bit of sun: don't block the light.

That is how it is with the song.

With those who hear it.

This horrible kind of pride is their sin.

It helps them to wrestle with solitude.

But perhaps it is less of a sin than a professorship in New Jersey.

For, of course, the battle will be lost forever, but we are in the line of fire.

The only place to be.

Doing what must be done, although we know what the echo will be.

The echo:

▪▪▪ 117

But . . . one must earn a living.

Earning a living is actually not difficult: I already know how to read.

That makes me privileged.

A flat, boring, hopeless, repetitive, futile life.

It's true.

But without stealing anyone else's life.

Lending myself money on occasion, yes.

Having no water or electricity on occasion, yes.

Wearing only one pair of shoes all year, yes.

Smoking cheap tobacco for months at a time, yes.

And trying to add a little happiness to the days of those who will follow, yes.

Nothing more.

Here, that is easy to do.

▪▪▪ 118

If you want something more: it could run into money.

You go along, sloughing off your conscience, little by little.

And no one can even guarantee that you will make it.

Life is an uphill battle, it's true.

But still, it is easy to come out on top.

All you have to do is remember that you are a second-class citizen.

That you must aspire to nothing but a second-class life.

And that, if you know how to read, you can buy into this second-class life.

What's more, you can always look out the window.

And what you see will console you—in the worst way, but it will console you.

In these environs, when the wind blows, and hunger and poverty, desperation and illness spread, they spread with a vengeance. So you console yourself.

You say: Good thing I'm a second-class citizen! And you eat your *salteña*.

In context, the dimensions of the problem can be reduced to an absurd degree.

It is not necessary to socialize: in two months you can

meet everyone who is anyone, get to know them well, and decide to forego these newly acquired friendships.

In another two months you will know everyone who serves the Beast, the weapons and means at their command, the things you can say and the things you cannot whisper.

And in another two months you can arrive at the conclusion that man's best friend is not a dog, but a book.

So, a room and a few books are enough.

A Roof: to pay for it, your life would be too short; if you build yourself a house—you privileged man—when you finish paying your monthly installments, your children will be planning their own funerals.

That is, if a revolution with a capital R does not come first and leave them out in the cold.

An Education: If you have a child who is not exceedingly dense, the chances that the boy will win a scholarship to pay for his entire education are nil: nearly everyone here who can read has gone abroad, speaks a bit of gringlish, and has visited faraway places.

So it is sufficient if you raise them well and teach them that survival is talent. If they have no talent, they can make an effort. And if they can't make an effort, they would be better off staying home and living the life they were born into.

Look at the statistics: No boy who was born even slightly intelligent has not managed to escape from here.

If he returns: he'll have his head to pay.

Belly: Lunch costs three cents in the Camacho market. This is paradise.

Only one place seems better: Tarija.

But that is a pipe dream.

The secret: always to remember that you are a second-class citizen.

▪▪▪ 119

Of course, there are difficult moments: moments when a second-class citizen is forced to remember that no one guarantees him his life.

No one guarantees his daily bread.

No one guarantees the lives of his nearest and dearest.

No one guarantees his dignity.

A second-class citizen is a dog. He is less than a dog.

He can be cheated, raped, murdered, tortured, quartered, made to disappear.

No one stands up for his rights.

At times like these, it is better to look the other way if what is happening happens to someone else; and to suffer and endure in silence if what is happening happens to you.

A second-class citizen can almost be compared to a Jew in the Warsaw ghetto.

The difference: everyone agrees that the death of the Jew in Warsaw was a crime.

Whereas the death of a second-class citizen is never a crime.

It is a dog's death.

It is legal and has never been a crime.

His death guarantees the sovereignty of his native land.

It does not matter if he was guilty or innocent of the crime for which he died: he is guilty of having been born where he was born.

And that is sufficient.

The second-class citizen knows it.

In that case, no one can help him.

And this is a truth that he prefers to forget.

He goes out, smiles, and cracks jokes.

He eats three *salteñas* and drinks a beer.

He thinks: This won't be my last eve . . .

After all, civilization still exists: they never let the corpses pile up in the streets.

▪▪▪ 120

What do I do with myself?

    Anything.

    Anything but take myself seriously.

TWELVE

▪▪▪ 121

There were four of us. One had been the Number One man in the time of the Patriarch a.k.a. The Monkey. He was an ex-Beast, he admitted later with a crooked smile. The youngest one's only crime was his family name: a name that was synonymous with the terror brought to this land by the '52 condottieri. The other one was a redneck. Maybe he was a rascal as well. I was the fourth. And there was one more, who spent only one night with us and let us sleep on his huge mattress.

The cell was another dark and dirty room, the walls of which featured the names and nicknames of the fatherland's saviors obscenely coupled with their mothers', in simple funny slogans. The room had seen better days: the ceiling still bore the bucolic country scenes some Frenchmen with handlebar moustaches had imagined. The floor was bared to the dirt foundation because the shiny wood planks of the previous century had been used for firewood to stave off the cold; the flames had left gigantic smoke tracks on the torn wallpaper. The windows had handmade frames but they were blocked off with bricks because they faced the street. There was an enormous stone in the room, close to dead center. There was a Louis XVI bed held together with wire, and the door was tall and narrow; it dated back to the time of Linares; it had no panes, just crossbars of rotten planks. The cell reeked of urine and human sweat.

When we walked in the rascal was already there. We looked at each other in silence because we did not know what to say. I leaned against the wall to listen to the light, cold, sad, and constant rain.

Some hours later, they brought in the man who had been *Número Uno* here before. He spoke, but not at length. "They're gonna beat us to a pulp," he said. "We're gonna get the shit kicked outta us." We looked at each other un-enthusiastically. My sphincter contracted. The rascal did not react. We did not speak, but I noticed his face. They've already started in on him, I said to myself, and yes, there were bumps all over his head and I saw blood stains on his nose. Looking at him fairly carefully, I thought that maybe he was a crook, as my grandmother, God rest her soul, used to say.

"I should know, because I was *Número Uno* here in The Monkey's time."

The Monkey here and now, I thought, remembering that his body guards, some thirty swarthy men, were lodged in the first yard, near the sewer where everyone goes to uri-nate. "If you're in here, that means they're gonna skin you alive. I used to be a guard here . . ." He looked about nervously, hoping we would say something, but we did not give him the pleasure.

Finally he fell silent and began to pace around the cell. A few hours passed and then the young man of the ac-cursed name was brought in. He was less than twenty. He was very well-dressed. That is, he had been, because he too was missing his belt, tie, and shoelaces. He did not say a word when he entered. We all looked at one another like people who arrive at a wake and find no friendly faces, no one to joke with. Later, motionless, we listened to the rain, all of us except for the former Beast, who began bothering one of the guards in the hope of finding an old friend in common to help him out of the little jam he was in. He tried for a while, but they let loose a mouthful of curses and he kept quiet, but continued to pace. He knew more than I did about the customs in the country of the Beast, and what our alternatives were.

We stayed there for one day and one night, freezing a little, sitting on the floor, smoking.

The rascal—we never found out if he was struggling to free his country or to deny that he smuggled drugs—left us every three hours or so and returned a while later, made softer by kicks and punches. He chose to keep his mouth shut and never talked to us. Only when the man of the accursed name wanted to share his blanket did he move over and sit at our feet, trying to cover himself better.

That was the night when, snoring like a tiger, a fetus of a victim, I rolled in my sleep onto the floor between my new friend and the rocks, because I was absolutely exhausted. A guard whose name I don't recall but whose face I will never forget, woke me by beating the chains against the lock, kicking the door, and yelling.

"And here . . . who's still in here?"

"I am," I said, still asleep, and the other one, who was stepping on my head with his foul-smelling boot, mumbled, "Sorry, Don Max," and half-dreaming, I answered my usual, "That's all right, son."

After he determined that the same men were in the cell as had been there that morning, he left, to go bang on other doors and bother the other poor wretches. But I was awake by then and the man of the accursed name was telling me, in his singsong eastern accent, how much noise I make when I snore.

"Shit; if this one calls me Don Max and I snore as much as ever, things can't be so bad, after all."

But my light mood changed abruptly when he told me that he had not moved his bowels for the four days since he'd been forcibly removed from his office.

"I'm afraid," he said.

I looked at him and realized that I, too, was afraid, and when he said, "We're screwed," I didn't say anything, because it was true. In his corner, *Número Uno* looked at us disdainfully, for there, too, social distinctions of color, dress, gesture, and speech reign; and the rascal covered himself with the skill and patience of those who are in the habit of spending uncomfortable nights in strange places. We looked at each other like the pros of any trade look at the rookies. It was three in the morning and, although I heard the doors being kicked, chains being rattled, and locks being banged all over the yard, I fell back asleep. I snored as loud as ever.

The kid shook me in the morning when they brought weak tea and a fresh roll, and I drank my tea out of a clean tin and ate the bread, tearing it in chunks with my fingers.

It was about nine o'clock already, there was no sunshine, and it was still raining. We went out to urinate. Since we were being held incommunicado, they put us in the cell, put the chain and bolt in place, and told us not to stick our snouts out; we fell into the routine: *Número Uno* silent and watching us with curiosity from his corner, the rascal coming in and out, in and out, puffier each time, but a tough nut to crack, and the kid and I talking finally, and slowly filling each other in on the how, when, and for how long, but never, never the why of our improvised friendship in the cell.

In the afternoon they brought me some blankets, cookies, and a mattress. I did not ask for my cigarettes. I had nearly resigned myself to my fate when I remembered my briefcase. My thoughts soured then and I sat on the floor, wrapped in my overcoat, looking blankly at the walls on which our national history was so profusely recorded.

▪▪▪ 122

Seven years earlier, still a visitor of Day, I'd finally got to the cabin between the lakes where the Man I wanted to visit lived, the Man whose voice I had followed from adolescence, the Man who wrote well, lived well, and was dying well, old and alone.

The walls covered with photographs, mementos, plaques.

A small kitchen, a wooden table, ice, a bottle of bourbon. The Man, his beard, his open shirt, his pipe, his big hands, lively eyes; time, which takes its toll.

The afternoon was languishing by the time I arrived to see him.

He knew I was coming; months before, I had requested a visit and nervously awaited his reply. I was lucky. He invited me to spend one night and two days with him.

So what did I learn from the Man? Nothing magical.

Just that no one can live another man's life, no one can borrow another's life, no one should write what he knows nothing about, no one should write for anyone but himself the first time; for everyone but himself by the final draft of every text. Looking at me calmly he also told me that it was a great sin to be a writer and not write, to always find excuses for not writing, and I lowered my eyes because he knew me.

I left as Sunday was darkening. He accompanied me to the town where he purchased supplies, showed me a panoply of rifles, recommended a .22, and went back to his house in his pickup truck.

But not before someone snapped a photograph of the Man and his visitor from Night.

Here I am now, remembering the tin cup of tea in my cell and the bourbon that I drank with the Man. He had taken the time to examine my work, to ask my friends about my hopes, to evaluate what, with any luck, I could do someday, and he decided that perhaps it was a good idea to invest a few hours talking to me about the writer's trade.

I pick up a magnifying glass and look at the face of the guy whose hand the Man is shaking. Unpressed shirt, wrinkled suit and tie, six years of wear and tear, but somehow he managed to win a meeting with his particular legend.

I still cannot convince myself that that guy is a pile of dung.

The Man would not have shared his well-lived life, his well-written work, and his richly decanted experience with a lump of dung.

But, nevertheless, this is what the Beast says I am, a lump of dung.

A lump of dung: all because my grandfather arrived in Mollendo in 1908.

▪▪▪ 123

That must be why, when I won the *Premio Municipal*—Purple Ribbon—in 1970, it, too, seemed like a lump of dung to me. And when I lost the other prize, the one for which I submitted my novel that was so personal that the judges decided to wring its neck, it all smelled like a lump of dung to me.

And the same thing is happening to me with local dung as happened to me with the sand at El Callao, which started to spread over everything until it choked me and I was buried in a black sea of sorrow.

Dung, dark green and compact, grows and thickens like a foul stench all around me.

I only have a few books left in me to throw them off the track before they decide, any moment now, that I am not necessary. To anyone.

They will decide one moment or the next, but they will decide.

In the final analysis, there are times I know that I have already died.

It's like what I've already written somewhere and cannot find: it's not serious. None of this is serious. Not even my death, the death of so many other lumps of dung, or our collective failure is serious.

It is a grotesque comedy, no more. An operetta in which the sea is lost, nationality is lost, hope is lost, tomorrow is lost, and all is lost, all but the absurdity of murder and torture, but the whole affair is still an operetta, sung by a thousand lumps of dung.

I am sick because I learned those words my father taught me before I could learn that man can learn, and I have been at it for forty stupid years, thinking stupid thoughts, analyzing piles of dung, chasing my eternal dog's tail, believing this unendurable situation must change even though it has endured now for a century and a half, living each day with the memory of the bullet in my father's chest, dung, the three hundred and seventy thousand hours he sacrificed, dung, my children's lives, dung, and the tragedy of my people, dung.

The worst thing of all is that looking at things in the silence of my room and feeling the world spin beneath my feet, at last I learn that hope has very good reason to elude all my thoughts. I feel certain that there is no reason for any change; I find that those who gambled on barbarity were right, those who put their money on robbery, murder, and exploitation were lucky, those who believed in torture and beheading came out on top; and the children of this continent will never wake up to a less clouded dawn.

The Beast has conquered me.

He has conquered us.

We are lost.

But since it's not serious, I cannot run outside to the street to shout it. I cannot relieve my desperation by talking to anyone, nor can I even walk through this door to tell my loved ones; this curse is even more terrifying when you possess the divine power to see what's coming next, that is, when you know how to read.

Here I am alone, waiting.

Alone.

Waiting for the end of an agony that will never cease.

▪▪▪ 124

How, then, can anyone dream up a tyrant's life, make him a senile grandfather, have him plant papayas in the afternoon and plant his seed in thousands of mothers; how can anyone describe his crimes of magic and wonder, all just to live in Barcelona?

I can't. I don't have it in me.

This is no time to nivolize. And the shit is just about up to my neck.

(Strange: it is not a curse that will die when I do; this song of mine is a lifesaver.)

▪▪▪ 125

Let's nivolize, let's nivolize.

She and I met one sunny day, at noon. I saw her, liked her; I'd like to marry her, I told myself, and I continued reading my newspaper because those were the last days of a hunger that Belaunde and Wilkinson owe me.

I was lucky, and managed to speak to her. I was luckier: I spoke well. I was luckier still: she remembered that I had spoken to her. To make a long story short: she is six feet away from me now, sleeping, as always, like a child, and my luck is holding out.

Not that it's been easy for her: she picked up the pieces of a journalist who had read and believed in Hemingway, she patched them, fit the pieces back together, and sent them back outside, nearly good as new.

As I said, it was what they call love, lucky me.

In time she gave me three distinct versions of herself in different issues: a pretty honey-colored blond who looked so much like a gringa that one day the doctor in La Paz asked how she got to be so blond just so I could remind him that my grandfather had arrived in Mollendo in 1908. Another, a catlike, quiet, clever one who cut me to the quick when he asked, at the age of two, where, in relation to our front door, the sea had been. And last, a third who denied having discovered America because she found it to be a tremendous prank.

It's not that I want to burden the audience with details, but it may be necessary to state that I love her, I need her, and, all things considered, God alone knows where I would be now if she had not come into my life. We both had to wage a terrible inner struggle before arriving at the tranquil armistice we have today. It was a long and hard struggle that we fought against everyone and everything until we recognized that, naked, alone, and sad, we were traveling companions on the road, however long or short, bitter sometimes or simple, the road that is this day, with the three of them filling our hours with laughter and smiles, surprises and wonders, simple good things and the wise, honest words children speak.

Fierce was her struggle to rescue me from the black cloud of sorrow I suppose I was born under. Brave and painful, her struggle to dislodge me from my only hiding place, coward that I am, the accidental escapes into the night, the dialogues with the monsters of the night, the ugly distortions of drink . . . Her love, however, even conquered that: one day, seeing her impotent rage, I decided that it was not fair to make her pay for my reading and here I am now, alone in the middle of the night, but knowing that she is sleeping six feet away from me, and putting my monsters to sleep so they won't hurt her anymore. It is not the final battle; it is a continuous war. As my myths crumble, I am more certain than ever that her love and generosity will also save me from the trap I fell into when life's blows overwhelmed me.

So it is, then, how love exists for me and has her name: Natalia.

Life for her has not been easy or smooth. To look at her you would not believe that she could fight her own battles. And yet she is strong, she is fair, and she is, above all, generous. In that, too, I have been fortunate, as you see, and I have to thank my stars, for in my heart I know that I did not deserve such good fortune.

So it is nivolized now: my monsters are internal ones; my happiness abounds, is undeserved and wondrous. Lost among nightmares and sorrows, my star has given me love and patience from my dear ones, and friendship and generosity from most of the others.

But she has been and is truly my refuge, my respite, my strength. She is here now, sleeping like a child. And because she is here, being who she is, nothing can ever seem too cruel or too absurd or too sad. She is always here at the end of every day and it is like the morning, when the world dawns lovely, new, fresh, simple. She has taught me that there are places in the world where the Beast cannot reach; she made me learn that goodness is strong, that happiness is always within our grasp, and that for me, love exists.

Only this strange destiny, which drives man to define his work, to begin his search and not find peace until he has begun it, is the cause of my anguish. That is why I am here now and not with her, though she calls me.

▪▪▪ 126

For we have made this with love.

It is not a palace, and perhaps all we have are small joys, a small garden, a dog, flowers, running water in the garden, fairy tales about The Little Red Indian Girl and The Big, Bad Balloon, Sunday outings to the country and nights of books, days of children's laughter and smiles; but we have made it with love.

We have made it with dignity.

We have made it all; we have few things, things that are humble, but they are ours, with dignity. I have nearly one thousand books. I bought my first ones in my student days when I taught English spelling for food money; the last one, a few days ago, with my work, modest, unimportant work, but useful. And she, who went away to school, fleeing the mercenaries of '52, with little more than hope, is a professional now. Recognized and paid as such.

She and I left this place ages ago, alone, sad, with nothing but an education, an alienating education that our parents purchased for us at a price of incalculable sacrifice. Provincials from the far end of the universe, we went out into the world and had to learn solitudes, eat solitudes, cry solitudes to make what we have made, naked, alone, sad but with dignity.

Look at the expressions on my children's faces: we have made these expressions, too, and we are proud because their expressions are clear, bright, happy, joyful.

Look at the few possessions we have: each has a story behind it and we earned each thing with our four hands; mine, which are so unsuited for practical labors, and hers, so deft and small, indefatigable in protecting, caring, sewing, and consoling.

What makes these things, which we love so much and were made by us with dignity, another pile of dung?

Who is he, the one who comes to turn our life—the life that we started from scratch and that is made of small tasks and small joys—into dung?

There is only one answer: she and I are a minority.

And I am foolish to let this terrible wound hurt me so.

A fool: not only was everything ruined before I was born; not only do they continue to ruin everything while I live isolated in a cave with my books; not only have they already dashed my children's hopes—they sleep peacefully tonight because no one has told them—but despite it all and against my wishes, when the sun rises tomorrow I will know I am feeling the sunshine in the very place I ought to be feeling it, I will know that I am doing what I have to do, and I will know that I am with my people, my Great Family, living the way my father taught me to live, without dirtying my hands.

I have nothing else left.

My father did nothing else, I am trying to do nothing else, as nothing else, when the time comes, will be left to my children; the same thing my father left me: the memory of his foolish honesty, the days of hunger with dignity he left us, and the pride I feel tonight in his honesty and his hunger.

I belong to this minority.

I did not choose it, but I am part of it.

I cannot change. Nor will my wife or children change.

We are the stupid minority whose only reason for being is to get robbed. The idiot minority who keeps a special corner of the house for books. The moronic minority who believes that it is educating itself when it seeks to square the circle. The disgusting minority who will always refuse to steal from the poorest people on earth.

And that is why I refuse to kowtow to circumstantial rulers, why I refuse to follow any old savior I come across.

Because I earn my bread, I don't steal it.

And I can say so, just as you read it.

I can write it, in a rage, as I write it.

Even if the Beast kills me tomorrow.

▪▪▪ 127

Mr. Chief of National Security, that is why I am not a Communist: I love my solitude so much that I believe in no one but myself; flocks will always gather far from my door; farther still, the herds.

Because to say what I say, I need no current or outmoded ideology.

Because, by Nature's whim, I was born to live and die alone and to bear with biting solitude unto the end.

I find refuge in my father's honesty, in the shield given by his honesty, and in the daily struggle we wage, my wife and I, my brothers and sisters, my few friends, and that refuge is enough.

Communist? Capitalist?

Victim, that is all.

I know what I am. I know why I am what I am: I picked my game of pinochle and its prize, children's laughter.

But I will never be a sheep.

And never a wolf.

Standing on the sidewalk, I watch young boys pass by, shouting.

I keep quiet and walk on. I feel like vomiting but don't. I go back to my cave and keep working. Modest, minor but useful work.

I earn my bread, I do not steal it.

And why should I want to be a Communist?

Or put my faith in capitalism?

Both are inventions that hope to shatter the parable about the camel and the needle's eye.

They will not succeed; they will not succeed.

They will not succeed.

▪▪▪ 128

And there will be some, I know, who will try to see in this attempt to reject in disgust the black dark sides of our common identity, a wish to renounce my own people . . . I repeat, I feel no hatred, not even toward those who are responsible for our sorrows.

I do not take anything back.

I only refuse to be part of the great complicity.

I accept my cross, which is to bemoan the cross my people must bear.

I find no way to lighten the perennial cross, but I do not contribute to making it heavier.

I also learned this in the cell: I am trying to be innocent of my death if they murder me and innocent of my life if I have to go on living for another two decades.

But: I do not take anything back.

I will keep chasing my tail, our common tail, while I have breath to breathe.

Not only because it is what I am cut out for, but also because I need to keep aiming to square the circle, to find an impossible end to this long torment.

Yes. I am not better or worse than my Brothers and Sisters.

They live in me, and I in them.

This is my world. And there is no other.

■■■ 129

Let's nivolize, let's nivolize.

The intensity with which nights of empty and hollow talk followed one upon the other made me turn to a doctor, to Western science, for a cure, a palliative for that distasteful social evil, existential angst and its derivative, drink.

The doctor did very little because he suffered from the same malady: no last can mold the human spirit to this earth like a foot to a shoe.

And thus:

The Doctor: I work with children and teenagers, I fight drug addiction, withdrawal, and I could tell you stories . . .

Me: It's just another freak show . . . No one buys tickets for these things anymore, no one cares to know, not even if admission is free . . .

The Doctor: So that's how we're feeling today, eh? How are you doing?

Me: I drink . . .

The Doctor: Well, one can't avoid it entirely.

Me: But they suffer; those who love me suffer. Sometimes I wish I had never been born.

The Doctor: Come, come now, it can't be that bad. Take these: one in the afternoon and one at night . . . Let's see what happens.

Me: What could happen?

The Doctor: You'll sleep.

Me: So you sleep?

The Doctor: Poorly. I am fighting a new war, a war against drugs. I could tell you some stories that . . .

Me: It's no use . . . No one thinks, no one reads: we are uncivilized.

The Doctor: But there's the satisfaction of getting the job done . . .

Me: We were born in the wrong place, at the wrong time.

The Doctor: We are all mistaken, yes, I know. The Flood, right?

Me: Which one do I take in the afternoon?

The Doctor: This one, and while we're at it, here's another one to take in the morning.

Me: Thank you.

The Doctor: Don't mention it.

■■■ 130

This is no time, then, to nivolize.

But, why nivolize?

Because, if I didn't nivolize, I would have nothing except for *Cheers!* and I would hate myself even more than I do now.

And if I left, I could not help but remember the girl from Peru; the memory of José Claudio would not leave me. I could never forget the children in this place. I would keep thinking about them, bemoaning their lives, cursing their luck, cursing mine.

What a mad destiny, to stew in my own blood.

What a divine path, lamenting uncontrollably and forever unable to do anything about it.

To chew my carrot because I cannot do anything else.

To know that I am here, that there is no better place for me, that this is it, and to know that our eternal anguish will endure until my own anguish ends as an end for this blind alley.

And to think I did not even choose this path.

Not able to pass through the forbidden door to the shadows because others think that I am necessary.

Walking through the streets, to earn my daily bread with my public-relations-man smile.

Such loneliness in my agony.

Me.

So here I am, bearing a difficult situation.

An unbearable situation that is enduring, still enduring.

Snap; the flags.

The flags . . .

Agitator #1: If you keep it up, you'll . . .

Me: Quiet, you; go shout at the boy who's just got out of school . . .

Agitator #2: God, in his infinite wisdom . . .

Me: Quiet, you; go shout in Hiroshima . . .

Agitator #3: Man, man, who forges his character . . .

Me: Go shout in Cambodia . . .

Agitator #4: The great demands that . . .

Me: Great heavens! I'm vomiting.

Me: Fold your Hands!

You: Oh, no, I'm vomiting.

And thus it continues.

Until the next flood.

THIRTEEN

And thus it is that, at any given moment, my moment of silence may strike; in the end I accept the echo, instinctively.

The echo:

Looking out the window, I see night is getting paler and it promises to be a kind, splendidly sunny day for my people. But the game of chance turns to fatalism, and nothing of what is yet to come, however frightful it may be, could have been avoided.

There will be no place to hide.

But through my books, books I have loved so dearly, I believe today, the dawn of my death, that I have become a citizen of the world.

I have been fortunate: the men who made the history of my time were my friends, and I shook their hands. In our small world, they were the men of '52. In the greater world, it was him. Him.

Only one man died before shaking my hand, but I was at his resting place and I heard his voice, a voice that spoke to many peoples, for his heart was too big to love his own people exclusively.

In our small country, a satrapy featuring dawns as stainless as the beginning of the world and cruelties as great as human absurdity, I was fortunate: my country gave me

Tamayo and in forty years, only one friend betrayed me. Who else could say as much?

Tamayo showed me about my death, and it is a death I accept: I may have to endure another two decades but I alone will know that I will endure them a dead man.

Tamayo endured his own death for a decade, and he is dead now, as dead as he was born. He doesn't owe anyone anything; no one owes him anything.

Out in the street, oblivious to all, children run to school. From here they look like faceless white dots.

It all must end so that it all can begin, so they say.

Thanks to my solitude, I am as old as the world.

▪▪▪ 132

Flaco: After twelve years of bourgeois life, what can you say?

Me: It's true. I can't say anything now.

Flaco: Well, finally: you needed a thousand days to accept silence.

Me: Yes, it's true. They needed a thousand days to kill me. I have finally found my silence.

Flaco: What?

Me: Nothing.

Flaco: Tell me the story about Ana.

Me: Huh?

Flaco: Anita Ana.

Me: Come on, I'll treat you to coffee.

▪▪▪ 133

"Yes, that's a good trick, but how did the five days in the cell end?"

They just ended. An idiotic interrogation, a month and

a half of exile, two scares, and back to the desert of echoes, to earn my meager living.

"Yes, fine, but how did it happen?"

Here is where this *nivola* ends.

For the addicts, the following pages have been added.

For those who know that staying up with a book until dawn is a foolish pastime, the *nivola* is over.

Thank you, ladies and gentlemen.

The show is over.

Musical finale.

And so, ladies and gentlemen . . . (applause) . . . the show of the week is over . . . (more applause) . . . The show . . . (wild applause) of the siren song!

Cut: Do you have a dead body at home? Go to Miss Maughins: one body, two coffins!

"What do you know!"

The show: click.

And that, my friends, is all.

▪▪▪ 134

Let's nivolize, let's nivolize.

One day, and because the third edition of my bestseller about Choqueyapu had just been published, I was drinking in a sleazy bar in order to listen to the raw material of my *nivolas,* when a shadow of a man hiccuped in my face, a hiccup big enough to kill a horse, and says:

"Oh, but . . . I know you."

I did not say anything, because every member of my Greater Family knows me, even if they have never seen me before. Three months earlier, some other guys who claimed to know me swore on their mothers that I was a Communist and threw two chairs and three empty bottles at me before we all ended up, you know, hugging one another, the best of brothers.

As I say, I am privileged because I know how to read, so I raised my index finger, called the waiter, and the shadow of a man was calmer once his glass was filled.

He drank as a person drinks who knows that at the bottom of his glass it's all over, and he looked at me slyly—his eyes qualified for Dr. Pescador's treatment—before repeating:

"Yes, man, I'm telling you, I know you."

You never know where the things you do when following your carrot are going to lead. For instance, innumerable taxi drivers have invited me for drinks in the Plaza del Estadio when I, under my own cloud, got into their jalopies and politely bid them: "Home, James, before the boss breaks my bones . . ." And the friendly guys working the dawn shift would say respectfully, "Let me treat you to a nightcap; I always read your articles, back then when they let you write." Thus, I would get home at six in the morning, making my wife, the angel who sleeps with her eyes half-open, go through hell once again.

But I was cautious with the shadow of a man. Who knows whether he has a dagger or a dirty handkerchief in his pocket?

Damn it, he was another one of the Monkey's men.

He was the Monkey man who, one Saturday night ages back, was guarding the car that belonged to one of the mercenaries of '52, the one I cajoled with the chicken and the egg game: Which came first, the chicken or the egg? I asked this man of the revolution, the militiaman with a rifle on his shoulder, on that night in the distant past; and after looking puzzled, like a chimpanzee faced with a computer, he said uncertainly: "The egg." The egg, you say? And there was no chicken to lay it? "The chicken, then!" The chicken, you say, before the egg was invented? "The egg!" . . . a long string of absurdities, helped along by a half-drunk bottle of pisco, and it went on and on until he sat down, toward dawn, a well-worn phrase, on the damp sidewalk and I, what with the chicken and egg game, crept into the shadows and stole his boss's car, the car belonging to the man who was leading his revolution.

Quite a comfortable car. Quite big. Quite a lot of buttons, levers, and little lights. I rolled the car down to the first bridge to Obrajes and then lit a match and watched it go boom! in the night, like a big firecracker.

And now, nearly bald, with bags under my eyes that are slightly, excessively sad, my hands gnarled, so to speak, now the shadow of a man looked at me, tamely waving his index finger:

"Which came first, eh? The chicken or the egg? You know?"

Woah. I had to touch my kneecaps just to make sure I wasn't still wearing knickers.

The demise of his boss's car became the undoing of the militiaman with the rifle on his shoulder. From armed guard he was demoted to hit man; from hit man to hatchet man; from hatchet man to a shadow of a man without father or mother—a bum, a thirsty beast of burden.

Hiccuping his "you knows," he enumerated his demotions.

"I saw your picture on your book, you know. And I remember your face."

Yes, well. Twenty-four years. I raised my index finger several times and the story emerged between his heavy hiccups that could have killed a horse. Shame shaded my memories in gray. I had created this Beast, who kept saying: cheers! to me.

Oh, what a sad story of "you knows," the shadow of a man.

Why retell it? My friends, in one way or the other, it is our story, give or take a detail, a disguise or two. The only good thing about tiring of trying to win a literary prize is that you do not have to be the least bit careful.

I put him to sleep by repeatedly raising my finger and bothering the waiter. I got sleepy listening to his long and sad story told a thousand times over, punctuated with "you knows" every so often. And when the waiter assaulted my wallet, my newfound friend, ghost of the revolution, was nodding out on the oilcloth-covered table.

There must be a hell, I preached. There must be one, even if I roast there, because someone must pay for your life, shadow of a man.

Before I had even learned to drink I had saddled him with my debt.

And, looking out of one eye at the corpse of the revolution, I learned that no one is innocent anymore; no one.

Neither I, who in adolescent mischief had created this Beast, nor the other man, who planted human bones in the valley, nor the other men who still play the easy game, taking advantage of the "you-know" fellows.

You, for example.

■■■ 135

It's downhill from here.

Just the scraps are left.

You have no reason to complain: it was over some time ago.

And if you are still here, it isn't because I invited you. Go to bed.

I'm going to spin a *nivola* of the fourth day.

The fourth day got off to a good start because some blankets were brought to me. In between the covers was a roll of toilet paper. I did not think of looking then, but I have it today. I mean, a piece of toilet paper that says, word by word: "We are fine. The children are fine. God willing, everything will work out. A lot of people are interested. Love."

From her.

I did not read it until I got back home because I did not need the toilet paper, but now I have the note. Appendix H.

Before dawn, the man with the big mattress was put in our cell. He was very young. Not even an adult. A heavy-set build, with a Mexican-style moustache. Wearing *chompa,* as we call such discolored sweaters, and dark pants. I was struck by his expression; he looked like a poor puppy: lost, eager, sad. Half curious, half shy, he looked at us, hoping to find friends. He had not yet lost his dignity, but he had learned to fear the Beast.

You, go to sleep; I am going to record the boy's story. He was born in Sucre, La Plata, Chuquisaca . . .

He got as far as college. One day, bored with the small town and its routines, he went in the street to shout. When he told me the story, he could not remember exactly what he shouted against. He remembered that his shouts were answered with bullets, that he ran like a rabbit back home, scaring his mother half to death, and that he hid in his bedroom.

They found him there a while later and took him to his first cell.

That night, the little city quieted down and his mother visited him. What have you done, my son, he told it, mimicking the weeping and the words spoken by his mother, a good soul as all the ignorant are. I don't know, the boy said he told her, he who had been brought up in a good family. I shouted; we all shouted. I looked; we all looked. They all ran; I ran.

He spent ten days thinking about what had happened and then they let him go.

Not for long. When the usual conspirators were getting ready to conspire again, the authorities decided not to be caught by surprise. They pulled the kid out of bed one day before dawn—like they did with me, I interjected—and put him back in the same cell. Twelve days, then they let him go.

Then he got to thinking that that was no way to live, getting hauled off to jail every time the usual conspirators conspired and the Beast was on a holiday; he told his mother that he would be better off elsewhere, because no one can live in peace with the Beast on his heels. His mother shared his fear: the world is big and wide, she said, and gave him her blessings before he gave his legs an airing.

The big, wide world was not so wide to him: he got as far as Tupiza.

And, staring into the sad flickering candlelight and smoking a cigarette, he said that he had found the world empty. He did not mention the love his parents showered on him, maiming him without his knowing it, nor did he recall the sweet subtleties his mother wove around him for fifteen years, but he said that yes, things got rough after twenty days.

And, he related, contemplating an empty world, he did what burros do: he let his legs carry him, and his legs carried him home, to his house and his room, where he slept peacefully in his old bed.

That was where the Beast's underlings found him. And once again he returned to the same cell. He was, or had been, in Guzmán's words, a marked man. There he stayed, ruminating on his bad luck, cursing the day he had shouted with the crowd, looked with the crowd and run with the crowd, and was found under his bed.

That afternoon his parents visited him and, frightened out of their wits, they asked him, from the other side of the bars: "My God, what did you do this time?" and they saw the truth in his eyes when he said: "Nothing. I am only living my life" and they left in silence, their heads bowed—I'm an only child, he said, as he related their visit.

Listening to the pleasant timbre of his voice at midnight and looking at his profile, his big hands resting quietly, his broad chest and childlike eyes, I knew that it was true: he wasn't hiding anything.

And as the candle burned down, he told of how he got to know his country by visiting the cells the Beast has built: Early one day he had left Sucre, La Plata, Chuquisaca . . . and that same afternoon he arrived in Cochabamba. "I heard voices from the stadium but couldn't see anything," he recalled; then one afternoon he was transferred from Cochabamba and was taken in a truck, through the frozen wasteland, to La Paz with its lights, mountains, snow, and crowds, which he saw through a nail hole in the metal siding of the butcher's truck he traveled in.

Finally, three years later, there he was, saying:

"They might send me to another jail, friends. Jails abound in our country. Could I ask you a big favor? My parents might come here any day now; could you tell them, if you know, what jail I was taken to from here? They can't move about so fast. They've been following me, but they always get there too late. All they find are empty cells."

And we said: Of course. Even if you don't get taken away. Your journey ends here . . .

The former Beast: Yes, that's the idea. I know; I was *Número Uno* here in the days of the Monkey.

He: No, there must be more cells.

He finished his story and shortly thereafter the Beast on duty kicked the door, announcing that it was time to go to sleep. Good night, we said, but no: the tips of our lit cigarettes danced in the shadows. His enormous mattress, where we all slept: *Número Uno,* the rascal, the kid with the damned surname, the boy, and myself, united at last, brothers.

Thus the fourth day ended, while outside it was drizzling.

■■■ 136

What are you looking at?

Go pick at your food like a respectable person.

What are you waiting for?

What are you reading?

What are you looking at?

Go eat your potatoes like a good second-class citizen.

■■■ 137

It is quite difficult; let's spin a *nivola:*

One beautiful morning I asked René, the swindler, if we could chat at the scene of his wrongdoing.

René is getting old. He has no one, no mother, no father, no dog who barks when he comes home. It seems he has a daughter, but sometimes it seems not. He lives alone, and, as I said, he talks like a character out of a *zarzuela,* and sometimes his brother, an olive-skinned man, vulnerable as a pregnant woman, accompanies him.

I never had a bad friend, not until René the happy-go-lucky builder came along, René the mestizo without ancestors or descendents. "He's a nobody, not a builder, not an engineer, not anything else," René-the-attorney told me. "The only thing we know about him is that he made off with some money from the Ministry of Labor." René, a no-good crook who stole six thousand dollars from me because I recognized his face from my childhood, remembered some nice things he had done when I was a teenager. My stupidity: because I remembered him as a friend from the golden years of childhood, I believed he was my friend.

And now, standing by his handiwork, looking at what our friendship meant to him, confirming the cruel extent of his bad faith, his spiritual meanness, his single-minded nastiness, the ruins of our great dream, a house to call our own, I looked at him and he looked back at me for a moment in silence.

"Well, pal," I said finally, "if this was the best you could do after thirty years in the business, I've been the victim of a blatant swindle."

"*Coño*. If anything needs to be shored up, I'll shore it up."

"This, my friend," Gastón, the expert, told me, "is the greatest swindle the world has ever seen, after the Spanish conquest; sue him."

"Your entire life as a builder will go down the drain; think of your professional prestige."

"*Coño*. Well, look, do whatever you please."

He turned around and headed over the green hill, down the path that is lined with eucalyptus trees. A barrel with legs, white hair, with bear-size arms, a dark monkey face.

I raised my hand, pointed my index finger, pulled back my thumb, and bent the mid-section: Bam, I whispered.

But I can't, as we know. I have three children; three.

So I went to see René, the attorney . . .

Well; yes, it is a stupid story. Stupid and boring, but I will have to nivolize about it: there exist serious suspicions that the number of Renés here is half plus one.

The Majority.

This simple fact means only one thing for the Greater Family: to express it I must have recourse to a Roman gesture, Caesar's gesture when he sent the gladiators to hell.

Coño. If René-the-swindler is the majority, there is no hope for the Greater Family; we would do better to close up shop and emigrate to South Africa. Because a lawless country is not a country. It is not a nation.

It is only for that reason that the audience must be bored with this story.

Then there are the photographs in Appendix E, an example, according to my friends, the experts, of a work of art in the world of swindles. They deserve to be chosen for posterity, if there still is such a thing.

I do not know why, but as I look at these photographs, the ruins of our dearest domestic desire—you know, middle class family, father who works eight hours a day, mother who works eight hours a day, people who try to present themselves in church with a clean Sunday face—the demise of our dream, of owning our own little house, it occurs to me that there is a grain of truth in the words of wizard-initiates: "a drop of water contains the sea; what is above is below; a grain of sand contains the entire universe." My small family's charred reams illustrate, contain, predict, and confirm the charred reams of my Greater Family.

And my gesture: naked hand, bam, is the gesture made by my Greater Family at all the Renés in our midst.

Why, then, relate the four-year battle we fought against René-the-swindler, observed with Olympian disgust by René-the-attorney? And what possible reason is there for telling the end of the story?

René-the-swindler has two houses, two cars, a few flashy suits, and a river in low-lying municipal land: he found a friend in City Hall who gives him the same spot in the same river every year, so he can build the same supports every winter against the same rainstorms that carry away the same cement blocks every year: René-the-swindler is, dear sir, a man of means.

And, one must admit, he knows the law.

René-the-attorney has done much better, as befits his education: to speak to him, you must speak of millions, and in dollar amounts. And I never talk of millions, only of thousands—few thousands and in peso amounts.

You: . . . What a way to tire me! There are swindlers everywhere, clever slick lawyers everywhere. The smart ones live off the fools, and you got the bad end of the stick, so keep quiet now.

Me: But aren't you another fool? Haven't you been cheated, too? Haven't you discovered that you can't do a thing to those who rob you? Unless you yourself start stealing, which you could not do?

Or could you?

This, brothers and sisters, is the principal obstacle to nationality.

The fact that no one, but no one, can take nationality seriously.

Let's see:

Why can I not, nor can you, perhaps, fight as boldly as the Russians did when they defended Stalingrad? Why can't we build our roadways at the same sacrifice with which the Germans rebuilt their autobahns? Why can I not, nor can you, perhaps, adopt a political ideology, any ideology, since they all have the same end, more or less: the promise of a future and better living conditions.

Stand alone in your room, with your hand on your heart; take God and Jesus Christ as your witness, and answer this question: Why can't you, perhaps, or I, opt for either one thing or the other?

Yes, I know: we all sing sotto voce and we all say Viva! from time to time, but let's try to be serious: Why? I persist: why?

Ask yourself: Are you prepared to die for guys like René-the swindler, for laws like our laws and elevators that don't work, telephones that don't ring, ministers who are laughable, and everything—everything? everything a never-ending, comic *zarzuela*?

Let's leave ideology aside; after twenty-five years of war, the Vietnamese booted the North Americans clear out of their country: let's not count the casualties or make invidious comparisons; let's simply persist: How did the Vietnamese get to see that singular day?

What made Ho the victor?

What do those men have, that we don't?

Where can we find it, that which we don't have, and which made Ho victorious?

▪▪▪ 138

Hey there, Beast; are you all right?

The family, all right?

Sleeping well?

I believe it.

It is wonderful to be a biped: innocence, like under-development, is a pinprick: a mental state, at most.

▪▪▪ 139

I can see his twisted hands, his broken, copper-colored claws.

I can see him, disguised as a petty bureaucrat, because no one understands better than he this war without quarter, without rules, without pity or pause.

I can see his face, a gray face because he lives at night, in the shadows. I can see his worktable, it looked like a toy desk, his papers in a neat pile. I can see the lovely, pristine, yellow, blinding sunlight on the old carpet. I can see his black tie. A touch of gold on his chest: an anonymous cross. But I always see his hands, hands mangled by a previous torturer in a previous cell, according to legend.

I can hear the shrill cry that he repeated over and over when he swept his useless, mangled hand across his throat and said:

"One more word, just one more word and . . . !"

And in his livid face marked by black spots, in his anger and hate, I see, time and time again, the little face of a child.

The child who repeats: "When they took you away, Mommy cried . . . and I, I sat in the corner and cried. I cried a lot."

They have killed me. One with his love, the other with his hate.

▪▪▪ 140

Two cells and three children.

In the end, fingers lose dexterity and typewriter keys raise dead echoes in the night. In the end, I look down a deserted little street and glance at the corner and try to imagine approaching footsteps, and I know that I hear nothing, that my imagination is flagging, that the world is made differently, that I am mistaken, and that nothing was right, and possibly, neither am I.

Thirty-five thousand hours have passed, I believe, and I have heard nothing. I shouted with all my might and no one answered. All I ever really asked for was a few spare hours to sit and type in peace, and it was not to be.

By day it is Caesar; by night it is Love. I am a prisoner. Two cells and three children. I was mistaken. That is all.

But, damn it all, I still hear it.

There, around the corner, it's right there.

FOURTEEN

■ ■ ■ 141

At daybreak on the fifth day, they kicked the door and called out the name of the man with the big mattress and the old parents who were always running late.

"I'm coming," he said.

He looked at us sadly, firm in his conviction that there is always another cell. We lit a candle. We watched him skillfully roll up his bundle of rags, as he had done a thousand times before. At his departure—he, a man whose stay with us had lasted all of twelve hours—we felt as sorry as if he had been a childhood friend. He left his cigarettes on the blanket.

"Don't forget to talk to my parents . . ."

A whisper, the clang of a door, and he vanished. That same night we heard the bootsteps of the soldiers who came to take away twenty more guys, the truck-size swarthy guys who had been the Monkey's bodyguards. "They're all going to Chonchocoro," said *Número Uno,* always well informed.

So dawn came as we were looking sadly at the tips of our laceless shoes.

If asked the man's name, I wouldn't know it. If asked what I remember about him, I would only mention his childlike eyes, scared and friendly, willing to be complacent, his broad back, his clothes.

He went to Chonchocoro, and his departure left us feeling more endangered behind that door. The previous night we had become casual friends, whispering jokes and kidding each other to stifle our anxiety. But without him, reality returned, brutal and meaningless.

One to Chonchocoro, another—Espinal, Luis—into a random ditch after being brutally tortured for more than ten hours in an open field; the majority disappear without a single scream; to us, then, our native land was a black, bottomless sea, peopled by cells and tombs.

"I can't move my bowels," said the kid with the damned surname all of a sudden.

"Today you will have to," I muttered.

The men came, kicked the door, and gave us the usual breakfast.

"What's the matter, it's no good?" repeated Huanca when we tried to return the tins of food, half-eaten.

It was drizzling; they took us to the usual corner to urinate. Awhile later, the rascal was taken out for his first beating of the day. I never asked him any questions. What for? When it comes to the Beast, things get very personal.

Número Uno, former Beast, still voiced his fears in low whispers, but he had less and less to fear; he knew he would get out of this one somehow. His mousey eyes belied his words, and when we looked at one another now, there was a big difference between him and us: he would walk out of there.

I remember the piss-hole, and I remember my constant, tremendous desire to smoke. I do not remember anything else. Nor did anything happen. It was cold, we weren't hungry, we looked at one another from time to time, unintentionally annoyed one another, and tried to read the comic books sent in to us from the outside.

The four of us sat hunched over in the cage because by then the weight of the cell pressed in on our shoulders.

▪▪▪ 142

It is as difficult for us to build a nationality as for me to locate the man who was taken to Chonchocoro. It is as hard for us to be able to offer something different to those who will follow as it is to establish a dialogue between the Beast and the man who was taken to Chonchocoro.

It is as hard for people to honestly believe in a dignified future as it is for the man who was taken to Chonchocoro to get to speak to his parents before they die.

Everything depends on two people.

You and me.

But, as we can see, there is nothing we can do.

▪▪▪ 143

If you are still with me, please be nice and please do not construe what I have just said as a condemnation of Chonchocoro alone; spare me the shame of naming the other cemeteries our politics have filled, the other monstrous crimes in our tradition.

However, don't be too nice.

Don't be so kind as to let yourself forget the many traces of our complicity.

If it so happened that I have lived in these times—and have suffered a little, just a little, as you know—don't think that I am only condemning those cells that I have seen. No one is innocent; no one.

And this story, as you can see, is nothing but a childish repetition of our history.

It wants to be a plea, a supplication, a request, a demand, a motion, an appeal, a hope that words like these will never again have to be written.

But, as any public official would say: Can't be done, they say.

■■■ 144

Perhaps there were others before him, but the one I remember is Remarque.

Ravic: it's his fault.

The Citadel. Then came the leopard, then the bells, and then *Ulysses*.

When I was sick, *La Peste*. *Barabbas*. And later, *Nausea*.

Then *The Old Man and the Sea*.

Here they are under my nose, so they don't let me forget them.

There were others but in the end I returned to the same ones. Perhaps there was yet another, one I don't see now. But never more than ten all together, never. Of course, there are one thousand and thirty-four. Every night I wrap myself in them as in a coat.

Nearly all of them are sad. Even the ones that laugh are sad.

Perhaps I am sad because they are sad; or perhaps I am sad, and they are sad, and so we understand each other. At least I think I understand them.

In the end, I learned.

It is as simple as absurdity.

And there is nothing else to learn.

Others will speak. The buzzards. They fall on their prey, disembowel and quarter it, wildly wave the leftovers as they jiggle their martinis.

They lord, they teach, they disembowel. They suggest, counsel, and condemn.

But they never recognize the one who comes and is worthwhile.

They write introductions, prologues, commentaries before, during, and after the text, trying to bathe in its light.

But they cannot. Ever.

It may take twenty years to learn this fact, but you learn it eventually.

You stop reading introductions, interpretations, commentaries.

And simplicity sets in.

A few years of journalism won't hurt, either. It will teach you to despise these ladies and gentlemen. Every day you see him do things and you can't help but learn.

Then, you must read the books again.

These books, I say. Texts only.

It is an art. It may take half a lifetime, but it can be learned.

Then, one must eliminate the other, the reader.

It takes a while longer but it, too, can be done.

And when it's done, the problem is solved.

Then but only then, you suspect you have learned. A little.

Another hunch dies then: this is not the best book.

The next one, perhaps. Or the one after that.

Which is great.

Because the best book, if it is truly the best, is the last one, after which there will be no more.

In other words, you will have died.

Of course, as in this case, it can happen that you are made dead.

Even though you walk around with your public-relations smile.

Then there is no book.

Never was.

Foxfire. That's all. And not even that.

Shadow, spark, shadow.

If that's how it goes, the last shadow should last awhile.

Two decades, let's say.

It can be endured. You have to make up your mind to live with the chains of love.

The secret is to express all your love until you run dry. And pray for it to last two decades. It might.

Then, the worst part is to walk through the streets, thinking foolish thoughts and suddenly to see a smile, a gesture, a glance from a friend who once was a part of your own realities.

It's difficult because the smile on his face, his gesture, his glance, all say the same thing: foxfire, foxfire . . . before they walk away up or down the street.

It's difficult because you know that they are not entirely correct.

Because the foxfire appeared when you discovered that you were capable of a love greater than self-love, and when you accepted a fate that looks mediocre, absurd, and disappointing to your friends, but logical and even natural to your enemies.

It is more difficult than letting yourself be killed, because it lasts longer.

It is more difficult than fighting and losing, because there are times when you lose self-respect.

But it is simple: you elected the quasi-peaceful days of someone else's childhood, almost like your own childhood replayed; and you paid for them in silence.

Treason helps to weave the cage of love.

It is a cage because it makes us vulnerable.

For the Beast, it is an easy fight, then.

He threatens the children of some, wields his power, shows his cells off, and polishes his tools, and naturally, he is in control.

Silence gives the Beast his life; it is his triumph.

Because the Beast triumphs and a day comes when everything loses its meaning.

There is no more "I."

No more "us."

Nothing but the Reign of the Beast, and a need to endure two decades.

It is all very simple.

The trapdoor closes. You accept it.

The foxfire appears.

The cage seems too restrictive for human life.

But perhaps it isn't, really.

Perhaps the next story about The Little Red Indian Girl will be all there is.

And perhaps keeping the Beast pacified is enough.

Craning your neck over the crowd, you look about and think that now it is abundantly clear: this is all there is.

There never was anything else.

In the end, it seems that no one listens to you.

Just this subtle bitterness.

And this immense desert.

▪▪▪ 145

The door was so low, you were afraid you couldn't pass through. But everyone passed through it. A student desk. A piece of blotting paper. A pen and an inkwell.

The window was not high, it was small. The sun was rising and projecting a stationary rectangle on the polished wooden floor. Calendars on the wall; Bolívar, Sucre, Santa Cruz, Busch. A tiny wooden chair. Everything spotless, impersonal, like a barracks. It wasn't an office. A living room, perhaps.

At the door, a sentry, a corporal. Inside, the Colonel.

It was five o'clock when they came to get me, I remembered, it was still dark out. I waited until nine. Silence in the waiting room.

The Colonel. Blank face, perfectly forgettable. Dark hair, with copper-colored skin. Hair grease. Short. Broad-backed, for his height. Traces of hair above the lip, mestizo eyes, impenetrable and deep-set. The cuffs of his shirt sticking out beyond his wrists. A gray suit. Blue tie. Black shoes. Slow gestures. A low, smooth, weak voice. A huge gold ring on a fat, broken finger. Twisted, deformed hands, clipped claws: his trademark in a thousand prisons, reminder of the rumored legend. Did you say his claws were mangled? Then, yes: it's the Colonel.

Later on, when I compared notes with other survivors, I would discover that the Colonel invented this bureaucrat: there were others as well, who were imitation Colonels, who used his name, used his voice, on whom the magic power of God was conferred when the Colonel wanted to be everywhere at once.

I walked in with the certainty that innocence gives to inexperienced innocents. I did not wait to be asked. I took a seat, just as I would do when I sold airline tickets and would sit down in a client's office. If only I manage to cross my legs and smoke a cigarette, I thought, I'll be all right: the world of offices is my world.

The Colonel did not meet my gaze. He read the file. His world, I would tell myself later, in the thousand nights of terror that followed, is not one in which looks or glances were permitted. It's a world of paper, of nothing but files. The Colonel read my statement. Accustomed to reading upside down as well as right-side up, I read the words I had dictated, letter for letter, in the twenty hours of illuminating dialogue with the interrogator.

No dialogues for the Colonel. His profession was to impose sentence, crucify the guilty, execute radicals.

"Colonel," I began my argument, "I am not a Communist and everyone knows it."

His rage exploded like a volcano and he tore the file in two.

"You are a Communist! You are a radical! The President is wrong . . . He is wrong: you should be shot!"

His claws shake. A nervous tic in his left eye. But he does not look me in the eye. His eyes are nailed to the paper.

"Me, a Communist? Who says so?"

Bad move. This is not a client's office. You are lost . . .

"I say so, you son of a bitch!"

"Colonel . . ."

"Shut up, pig!"

The sentry nervously opens the door. He readies his rifle.

"Nothing's the matter, corporal."

He is seated again. He reads a piece from the file. He puts it down. He looks at the wall, a lithograph of Simon Bolívar. He shouts, furious.

"One more word, just one more word and . . . !"

He draws a fat, twisted, square-nailed thumb across his throat.

"You, and your . . . your little ones . . . Understand, radical?"

I understood. A slight tremble and cold sweat. I understood.

"And now, get out of here, you prick!"

▪▪▪ 146

And now when I try to remember it, I can't.

I can't recall it or recount it because I do not believe it.

I have lived it, I have experienced it, it has tormented me for many years, and I do not believe it. I cannot believe it.

I cannot believe it or tell it because it is too stupid.

It is so stupid it makes you want to vomit.

It makes you sick with disgust.

It tempts you to want to renounce human fellowship altogether.

If Atlas, Mr. Paez, and the Colonel control human experience, then it is necessary, it is imperative, it is compulsory, to disavow humanity.

I refuse to repeat it. I can barely remember it.

Now I understand the people whose fingers, tongues, hands, genitals are cut off by the Beast. Those who mourn for a relative, a friend, or a disappeared child. I see why they did not elect vengeance, why the Beast moves, unpunished, among us.

His stench forces us to forget him, to reject him. Impressed on our minds is the need to deny him, to destroy the memory of his burning slime on our naked skin.

That is why we disguise Hitler as a dirty old witch and use him to scare children who won't go to sleep.

That is why the Beast never dies: the Beast lives on our compulsion to ignore him.

I, who was under his thumb, who was defenseless, frightened, assumed dead by many, disappeared and negated, today try to testify against the Beast, and now, right now, when I should do my duty, silence prevents me: disgust and disdain overcome me.

I see myself choosing to deny his existence.

I don't forgive: I am disgusted and my insides are churning and I avert my eyes.

I cannot remember, that is all. I do not want to testify now, not right now, when I ought to be offering testimony.

Though I know this makes me the Beast's accomplice.

I hesitate, have a drink, light a cigarette.

One never talks about these things, I think. No one tells these stories.

I remember people who speak of the Beast from experience, and on the street they mention it in passing, as if relating a trivial incident.

Why defile life even more by talking about how incredibly, inconceivably, colossally stupid the Beast is? I say to myself.

And that is how I discover this very night that I refuse to perpetuate the Beast.

I cannot remember what happened that night, when I began to give my biographical data.

One day, someone will find the paper it took the Beast twenty hours to fill out; someone will glance at it and smile: good material for the eternal comedy.

Good tombstone for so many dreams, wishes, speeches, and hopes.

Here I am, then, I have been defeated.

I tried to point my finger, to accuse, condemn, and demand punishment, but I cannot. All I feel is anguish. Disgust. And shame.

I want to yell: "Forget it; forget it: it was nothing . . ."

But the Beast feeds on this forgetting and grows stronger.

I cannot seek justice, take revenge, or appeal my sentence: all that comes out of me is this awful, "Forget it, forget it . . ."

That's all we can do, I suppose, is forget him.

Erase the memory of his assault, deny his divine stupidity, try to forget so that others will forget and so that things will seem better; perhaps if they seem better, they will begin to get better.

In other words, perhaps we can believe in a tomorrow.

Yes. It is just another excuse, I know. But I feel so defenseless that I have no alternative. For, I suppose, if I decided otherwise, I would be identified with the Beast.

And to my mind there is only one thing worse than being his victim: it is being identical to him.

So, then, Brothers and Sisters: let's forget the Beast.

Although he is undoubtedly busy at work tonight, too.

▪▪▪ 147

After saying such things, I should admit that the days of transparent friendships ended.

Because after forcing oneself, for clear reasons and obscure motives, to get to the point of needing to expose the Beast, needing to demonstrate, indict, insist that he be sentenced like a common criminal, and then finding that one cannot even formulate the complaint, one must accept that from now on it will be difficult to open the front door and smile at strangers and say:

"Come in, friends; please come in."

For you have not done right by your friends. You have not honored the dead. And you are afraid of strangers.

The Beast can use anybody's face.

That is his power, his curse.

He has shown me the world as it is. And it is his world.

I will never be able to accept his world. Never again will I sleep soundly. I will not be able to trust a soul. Never again will I be able to conceive of my life as moments of reading, of dialogues, of silent and hopeful searching, of beautiful, subtle, surprising, and harmonious visions, of partial but luminous answers to the eternal who am I, where do I come from, and where am I going. Never.

Such is the power of the Beast.

And I recall:

The young reporter, on television: Why don't you write another book? Are you afraid of the critics?

Me: No, I am afraid of savagery. And I am alone.

Alone, because there is no place for me.

I should never have been born here.

I should never have existed here.

I am cast off; not necessary.

I am a shadow here, with no reason for being.

I find all this now, when I cannot leave, cannot take my life or let myself die. Now that I must go out in the street with my public-relations smile to pretend that the Beast does not exist, because I need to earn a living.

Now, when I still must try to justify what I do—

unimportant, unsubstantial things, to others' minds—
warring with myself, so I will not hate anyone, will not look
down on anyone, so that I can learn to live in the Beast's
world without being infected by his burning slime.

▪▪▪ 148

For if I give in to that easy temptation, all will be lost,
not only in this business, which is for half-wizards, half-
madmen, but I will also lose the only thing I have left, the
thing I am fighting to hold on to: this shield that makes me
superior to the Beast because I do not hate.

His victory is this immense desert and this subdued
bitterness.

I see my victory coming, I feel it, sense it here, although it is just being born.

Before me stretches a black, limitless emptiness, stray
sparks.

My superiority consists in my inability to kill him; his,
in his ability to kill me.

And the Beast will.

But it will be too late, I think.

Caught between so many contradictions and gripped
with terror, I believe I have found my way at last.

Yet another paradox.

▪▪▪ 149

It is dawning and I glimpse the sad curve of my father's
back. He is drawing, as he always did, on onionskin
paper, for the men who want the dimensions of their land
measured.

A child, I am reading. I look at him every so often.

I tell myself: he is building my days.

The times will be different, I will see his work.

I will see the sunlight on the sea, our sea.

I will meet the men who gave dignity to life.

That's what I told myself, as a child.

It wasn't true, now I know: he died in pursuit of his song, believing in better days.

The time has been consumed.

Nothing has changed.

The Beast reigns.

How right Alvaro was when he argued: "Don't write, man. Don't stick your neck out for anything. Truth is a deadly sin. Keep quiet, live and learn."

No men are sadder than those who plow the sea.

There is no courage greater than the courage of a man who fights a losing battle, but fights it all his days and can still say that he hates no one.

My father.

Let me repeat the words my father taught me: I hate no one.

To hate would be to insult myself.

But no one owes me anything for this.

▪▪▪ 150

When I left long ago, I did not leave because I had attempted to assassinate the Monkey, as some legends would have it. I left because I discovered for the first time that I should not have been born here, I should never have lived here.

The night I left was the night, I believe, that I made the first decision of my life . . . because that night I truly began to live; previous decisions had been others', which I adopted as my own. At the time, I thought some were mine, but no: they resulted from decisions that others had made for me.

But I decided to return.

How could I resist the temptation to return, when my blood, my own blood, was calling me?

The idea of returning made me sick; I trembled and urinated on the plane's stairway; a mad shiver took hold of me, for I guessed what lay in store, I saw it all, felt every blow, predicted the bitterness, but I returned because I had learned a love that was greater than self-love: "You never did anything for them," Natalia said. "You never even tried; you never did anything to be of service, and you leave nothing behind . . ." Well, now: don't say that I didn't try. I tried and tried and wasted twelve years trying.

The Echo:

Now I must adopt another decision to reinvent my life again.

I will accept my death in the Beast's world, this death and this silence imposed by the Beast, and I am going to wipe out his world with a single stroke, this world that I cannot accept, cannot describe, cannot recall; nor do I want to recall it.

I am going to leave again.

I know that for the Beast, the world has no borders, so my trip will take me far, far away. And I know the Beast will harass me every day, so I will have to build a strong world of my own; I also know that I shall remain here, rubbing elbows with the Beast time after time, so I must learn from the Beast and must renew my public-relations smile, a powerful weapon.

I do not know if I can, but I hope to bring those I love into my invented world; they are outside now, still laughing, because we have bought them some time, but later on, they must make their own decisions.

As they, my family must, so must . . . My Family.

I will be waiting for them, though I have left by other means. If they look for me they will find me, and that will be a partial victory. If they listen to me, I will be useful to them. I do not say that they should follow me, only that I will be useful to them.

So I am leaving now.

Another moment of their crystalline laughter, and I sink into silence.

The sun's ray on my Mountain, and I plunge into the shadows.

He killed me, but too late.

TOO LATE

The Beast hated me in his thunder and power, ready to burn me in his hate.

The Beast looked through me and forced me to look back.

And when his burning slime covered everything, only one thing remained untouched.

There it was, in his eyes.

With no clothes to protect me, with no hate whatsoever to use to fend off his burning slime, standing naked before him, I discovered it.

I perceived it, finally, when we were face to face, a spark of terror in his expression.

For the Beast heard it. I heard it.

I heard its simple certainties ring while he moaned, groaned, struck out, and sputtered in anger.

I heard it, I heard it, and I knew what had been, what was then, and what was to be.

For the Beast hears it constantly.

Because its murmur made his look of hatred turn to fear from the first morning I was his captive.

A fearful, deafening whisper that the Beast could not destroy.

Blinding in its patient wrath, an inescapable, unavoidable, eternal plague on his houses and his head and his mangled hands.

Man of little faith . . . Man of little faith:

The Echo.

The Echo, objecting. The Echo, getting louder.

The Echo, tearing through the Beast.

The Echoes.

So many of them.

The low, insistent voices from afar broke down the bolted door of my dark cage.

Weak voices united in a chorus of anger, registering their protests over their insulted dignity, over my deprived dignity.

Quiet but persistent, persistent demands from afar, like clear particles of light . . .

Words, phrases.

Simple words.

Humble words, repeated over and over and over by distant voices, deafened the Beast.

They paralyzed his claws.

They froze his burning slime.

They drowned his hate-filled screams.

They silenced him.

They pushed him back to his black cages.

They defeated him.

The Beast could not destroy me.

It was not easy.

An act of faith was needed, once more.

This act of faith.

This morning is fresh and transparent.

I am shut inside, fighting the typewriter, fighting with it and against it.

I read over my work and find, as usual, that it is impotent, mediocre, limited.

Outside, the children are playing with the dog.

Mountain water sings in the garden.

There are women's voices, and bird songs, off in the distance.

And you, Brother, are even farther away, but you are there.

I think of you and a crystalline joke is born in me.

This is what happens, Brothers and Sisters, because you have been the butt of a well-intentioned joke.

You were part of it, are part of it, and will be part of it, so the joke is fitting.

It is very important to me, though you may forget it.

This pun written not for you, but with you.

If you paid no attention to my courteous and less-courteous invitations for you to leave, I must tell you that, as you go reading line after line, I go reading along, too.

I needed you.

You were, are, and will be part of it all, and no one is innocent any longer.

I needed you to carry out this act of faith.

To commune with you and you with me in this act of faith.

I needed you to clear the brush along the roads I have taken you, the paths, alleys, and byways, places where I could not have traveled on my own.

I needed you so I could whisper in your ear, to tell you that the Beast did not triumph.

To tell you that I found a weapon to defeat him.

The Echo.

Your voice, Brothers and Sisters.

I needed you to convince myself that I have defeated the Beast.

That he may inflict the same terror and fill me with disgust again, but that I have defeated him.

That I know he can do as he pleases now, he may ruin me or kill me.

But I have defeated him.

Because now it is almost as though I cannot die.

I needed you so I could tell you that the road has been long and hard, that I have ripped the surface of silence, that I shall try to find you again, that I will pretend to be ignorant of your destiny, but I won't be: I have defeated the Beast and know now that there is no room in you for both of us.

I wanted to let you know of my good fortune in this sordid struggle, which you surely have followed with great difficulty and generous patience.

Perhaps I also wanted to drop a hint, to invite you to wage this same fight against the Beast, to fight it with me some day, shoulder to shoulder. So many children are yet to come . . .

I need you, too, Brothers and Sisters, to let you know that you can attest to my triumph, by participating in it.

Like an echo of the keys as they write these lines, you will know that I have triumphed, because my voice has reached you.

And you can vouch that I have triumphed because you hold in your hands the ultimate paradox, the siren song that is throbbing in this the last period.

La Paz, Good Friday, 1979